Our
Good
Name

Our Good Name

A Novel by Catherine Marenghi

ARCH STREET PRESS

First Arch Street Press edition: May 18, 2022

ARCH STREET PRESS, ARCH ST. PRESS
and colophon are registered trademarks of Arch Street Press.

For information about special discounts for bulk and nonprofit purchases, please contact Arch Street Press: sales@archstreetpress.org.

Book design by idesign communications
Cover design by idesign communications

Library of Congress Cataloging-in-Publication Data is available.

ISBN: 978-1-938798-39-9 (paperback)
ISBN: 978-1-938798-46-7 (e-book)

This book is dedicated to the people of Milford, Massachusetts,
who birthed me, schooled me,
and who, after my long absence, welcomed me home.

A good name is better than precious ointment.

—Ecclesiastes 7:7

Art is a lie that makes us realize truth.

—Pablo Picasso

Some ask why I think on the past
but, like these spiky plants, tilting greenly
at aging stars, I can't unfurl, can't breathe
into this word at the tip of my tongue
without remembering where I come from.

—From "Agave" by Kathryn Jordan

A Letter to My Grandparents

Dear Stefano and Celestina,

We've never spoken. But I have given you and your family voices with which to talk to me. I hope I have listened attentively to what you might have liked to say.

I have taken the bare bones of your stories—dates, places, names—and fleshed out the connective tissue in between with tales that I imagined, told in many voices. I have swallowed you whole, passed you through the filter of my mind and memory, and made you a part of my body.

My writing mars and changes you. I am sorry for how little I really know of you.

Who will be lost in the stories we tell ourselves? Facts fade and shift. Newspapers misquote, and text is lopped off to make way for other stories. Handwriting is badly transcribed. Archives have missing pages. Mold and fire consume what is left.

History is slanted. The experts betray us.

Only our stories are true. Only our stories remain.

Your loving grandchild

Part 1

The Old World

Marianna, 1910

You. Over there. You waiting for someone? You come to see me? No?

The light from the window behind you make you face dark. Come, you, sit close to my bed. Now I see you better.

I have a story to tell you. I tell you the important part first, in case you in a rush. Here's what I want you to know.

Death rides a bicycle.

You hear what I say? *Death rides a bicycle.*

I tell you why. You have two, three minutes?

You. You look so young. You don't know. Your mamma probably came here like me. From a little village, like I did. My village is Varsi. You never hear of it, no? Varsi, in the north of Italy. Where the green mountains touch the sky. I remember the little fortress near our village. We call it the *rocca*. And the church of San Pietro Apostolo. That's where I marry my Luigi.

When my Luigi go to America in 1894, he leave me behind with three little babies. Four, five, eight years old. My Celestina, she the oldest. It's good to have daughters. They take care of you when you get old. My Celestina—someday, I will lean on her like a cane.

Then the middle one, Giuseppe. He the strong one. So serious all the time. But my baby, Giovanni, he the best one of all. What a beautiful boy. His face—like a sweet plum. His body still like a baby, shape like a pear. I call him my Nino, my Giovannino.

When my Luigi go to America, he go to a place in Massa-… Massachoo-… I never learn how to say it. I stay in Varsi. I live with my mamma. In the old days, she watch my babies while I go work in the rice fields—the *risaie*. You don't know about the rice fields, do you? In the land between the mountains, where it is flat and full of water. All the women, like me, the *mondine*, work in the hot sun all day, up to our knees in water. My mamma was a *mondina*, too, when she was a girl.

Then, by and by, my mamma get too old to watch my babies. She need someone stay home, take care of her. Like she one of my babies now. When my Celestina is ten years old, she watches her little brothers and my mamma, too, so I can go work in the rice fields.

We wait five years, five long years, for my Luigi to send for me. He work hard in America every day, in the place of heat and metal where they melt the iron, make machines. He say it hot as the fires of hell. In summer, he work the people's gardens, too, with shovel and hoe. All the work he can get. He save up the money little by little, *a poco a poco*.

Then one day, we get the letter from Luigi. I don't know what it says, but my little Celestina, she the smart one, she read the letter to me. It says, '*You come to America now.*' My Luigi, my Lui, he sends me the money. Enough for four tickets on the boat. And one American ten-dollar bill. He tells me to sew it into the hem of my skirt.

I don't want to leave my mamma. For Lui, it was different. His mamma—I remember her name, Maria Pettinati—she died giving birth to Lui. He was her first baby, too. She just twenty-two years old. The church had a baptism for baby Luigi and a funeral mass for his mamma, all on the same day. His papa, Antonio, I think he go a little crazy. There was a girl, Rosa Tibaldi, who came every day to take care of the baby while Antonio worked. But Rosa was a pretty thing, and next thing you know, she's sleeping in Antonio's bed! Poor Luigi's mamma, her body not even cold in the ground, and not two months after they bury her, little Rosa is carrying Antonio's second baby!

So Lui's papà, he has to marry Rosa. He has to. Five months after his first wife dies. But little Rosa, she had her misery, too. Her first baby was born dead. And then she has one, two, three, four more babies. But the last one—she died having that baby. Poor Luigi lost two mammas before he twelve years old. *Madonna mia.*

But I get back to my story now. My Luigi is in America. The year is 1899, and the time has come for me to go, too. I think, *things will be different for me.* Now I can be a real lady. No more work like a man in the fields. No more rough hands. I go to America now. I have one cardboard suitcase, and I bring my good black dress, a picture of my mamma, and things for my babies. I will have a nice house in America, and my children will play, not work, but play like the American children do. I can buy a nice bolt of good cloth, make new clothes for my babies and me.

I will live like a queen in America.

When the oxcart come, I climb on with my babies, and we try to get comfortable on the straw. It scratchy and bumpy. We take the road west to the train station. I don't know why, but my Lui tells me to take the train to Napoli and take the boat from there to America. I want to go north, to *Francia* like he did, but he say this way is better. Maybe cost less money. Maybe easier on the babies.

When I get to the train station, I brush all the straw from my skirt. I have to step on the train like a lady. Anyone see straw on my skirt, they think I'm a *contadina*, a peasant girl from the farm. No more.

All the way to Napoli, I feel worry. I don't want to sail on a boat with all the *Napoletanos,* the *Sicilianos.* The people of the *meridionale.* Those people not like us. The Arabs come to *Sicilia* long ago, mixing their blood with *Sicilianos.* Their blood is black ink. They dip Sicilian hair into their black Arab ink. The men have veiled heads like women. They drink tea through a sugar cube in their teeth. The Arabs gave their sugar to Sicilians. Everything there is too sweet. That's what my mamma always tells me. I never seen an Arab before, but that's what she tell me.

You there, you still listen to me? I see you sit there. Your eyes get heavy. My story is not too long. You listen. Not much longer.

I remember sailing on that boat. *Che miseria!* They call it the Massilia. Black and ugly. Worse than the oxcart, where you can smell the backside of the animals as they pull you. This boat smell worse. I wish I had some rosemary and mint leaf from my garden to put in my nose so I don't smell the other people. I want to stay in my bunk bed all day, with my little baby Giovanni next to me. But he not so little anymore. He nine years old now. He wiggle when I hug him too tight.

Filthy, smelly boat. And the food—they call it food—not fit for animals. I want to leave my bed and get some air, some ocean air, but the people are so many, and it is too cold. I stay in my bed almost all the time. Weeks go by.

That's all I want to say about that boat.

When we get to America, I watch the other passengers so I know what to do. First, we have to go to an island, they say. Here the water has a bad smell, like dirty socks. We stand in lines. They poke us and push us and look close at us, like they are buying a piece of fruit at the market and are looking for rotten spots. All the time, I think about my Luigi. I tell my little ones, "Be brave, don't worry. Papà waits for us."

When we get to our train, my babies sleep all the way. Giovanni sleeps on my lap, and Celestina and Giuseppe sleep at my sides. They make a pillow of my shoulders. But I can't sleep. I don't want to miss our stop. I write down the name of the town so I don't forget. Milford. Milford.

Just like he promise, Luigi wait for me when we arrive. But I don't recognize him. He look like a stranger. His felt hat is old and dusty, and his shoes are full of holes. I can see his toes come out of his shoes. And his big black moustache has white hairs. He just forty years old. I don't see him for five years, and now I have to sleep in the same bed with this old man. I want to sleep with little Giovanni, like I always do. But Luigi says no. It not good for the boy. So I do what my *marito* says. He's a good man, work hard all the time. I lucky to have a good husband.

Luigi tell me he find a nice little apartment for us, but he want me to have a house someday. And we do. In a few years, we have a pretty white house on Hayward Street. Just like Luigi promise me.

By and by, I have another baby girl. Lui say we name her Maria after me. But I don't want her to be like me. She my American baby. I want her to grow fat and rich and always have plenty to eat. I will teach her to cook, and she will never be hungry. Some day she have a *trattoria*, a nice restaurant, and feed all the people in town. You'll see.

But this is what I want to tell you about. My little Giovanni, he not a baby anymore. He get big and tall. I want him to have a bicycle, just like all the American boys have. I work hard in the straw hat factory. I make money and buy him a bicycle. A new bicycle. Then I write a letter to my mother in Varsi, and I tell her: we now a rich American family. We have a new bicycle. All the rich people have new bicycles.

It is ten years now I am in America. My baby Maria is seven years old, plump and pink as a little pig, and pretty, too. My boys are so big and handsome, and my Celestina, she already married. She find a nice boy named Stefano, red hair, north Italian boy from Pereto. She have two babies already, one more on the way. They make a nice house right across the street from me, so I can watch her babies grow. And my middle boy, Giuseppe, they call him Joe. He engage to a nice north Italian girl, too.

It's 1909. That's the year I don't forget. My baby Giovanni already work in a factory like a man. Everyone call him Johnny because we in America now. Seventeen years old. He ride his bicycle to work every day, the one I buy for him.

Hot summer day in July. That's when they come to my house to tell me. A man in a car hit my boy on his bicycle. East Main Street, they say. They take my boy to the hospital. Broken ribs, broken lung. My Giovannino, my beautiful baby!

I don't believe. I don't believe. I go to hospital. I see the doctor's face and I know. He not have to say a word. I scream. I scream at him, "Why did my boy ride a bicycle? No more bicycles! You tell all the mothers, no bicycles for your babies! Only death rides a bicycle! Death rides a bicycle!"

They give me a needle to calm me down. I wake up in a hospital bed. I ask the nurse, "Why did I come to this country? Why did we come so far? Why do I want my boy to be like American boys—why? If we stay in Varsi, my boy still be alive. Do you have little boys at home? Do they have bicycles?"

I don't go to the funeral. I can't watch them put my baby boy in the ground. I think, maybe if I don't see it, it won't be true. I stay home all the time now, and I wait. I wait for my baby boy to come home.

By and by, a man come to our house. He say he from the U.S. Census. The government want to know how many people in the country in the year 1910. He want to count the people in my house. He see me, my husband Luigi, my girl Maria, and my big boy Giuseppe with his new bride Maria Malvermi. They all live in my house. He ask each one how old they are, if they speak English, if they read and write.

But I say there's one more. There's my Giovanni. Don't forget Giovanni. He ask how old is Giovanni? How many years has Giovanni?

I say, "He has no years! No years! None!"

I make him write it down. And can you believe it? He wrote it down on his census paper: Giovanni, zero years. No years!

Now you see why death rides a bicycle? I am happy you listen to my story. You're a good girl. You remind me of my Celestina. She my oldest girl—she'll take care of me some day when I'm old. My sweet Giovanni—he's the best one. He's the sugar cube in my tea. Did I tell you that already? I think I have another boy, and a girl, too. I can't think their names now. Do you know my Giovannino?

What do they call this place? Westborough? A hospital? I don't think so. Is that what they call it? They strap me to the bed at night, and I can't move. This is not like any hospital I know. No one ever get better here.

Celestina? Did you say your name is Celestina? That's my daughter's name, too. Maybe you know her?

Stefano, 1879

One day I asked my father, "Why did you leave Italy to come to America? Why?" He answered, "When you're hungry, my child, straw doesn't fill your stomach."

—*Evelyn Bontempo, an immigrant's daughter, Milford, Mass.*

"Rosso, Rosso, wake up. Get out of bed. I need water to make polenta tonight. Help your sister get the water."

My eyes have not yet shaken off the night's sleep, and the first morning light has yet to scale the tall mountains looking down on our village. It is too dark to be thinking about anything but sleep. My body has made a dent in the mattress, carving out a space in the *scartossi*, the corn-husk stuffing. The warmth of my body softens the brittle husks.

"Mamma," I moan through my pillow, "why do we have to have polenta for dinner? Always polenta. Polenta, same thing all the time."

She slaps me hard on the head.

"Rosso! You don't talk to your mother like that! You're lucky to have food at all! Your papà and brother work like mules all day, just so you can have something in your belly!"

"My name is not Rosso! I am Stefano!"

"*Vai, vai,*" my mother interrupts. "Hurry, so you get back in time for school."

My sister Giuditta is watching and gives me a sympathetic look as I slide to my feet and reach under the bed for my shoes. I stumble outside to pee and come back inside to splash some cold water on my face from the basin near the door.

"You mustn't pout, little brother. You're lucky to be a little Rosso with your pretty red hair. All the girls will love your pretty hair and pretty pink cheeks, little Rossino."

I hate it when she pinches my cheeks hard, and I feel my face redden. I can't help it. She hands me a bucket and we start walking to the village fountain together.

"You know, Rosso, our mamma had another baby Stefano long ago. He died when he was just three. That was a long time before you were born. She loved her first little Stefano. That's why she doesn't like to call you that. The name makes her heart ache too much."

"You remember him, Giudì?"

"No. I wasn't yet born when he died. And mamma's first baby was named Pietro, before your big brother Pietro was born. The first Pietro died when he was six. So, you see, you and your big brother are both named after precious little boys that Mamma lost long time ago."

"That made Mamma sad?'

"Yes, my little brother, very sad. When I was born, Mamma was wishing for another boy. A family needs sons, many sons, if they want to live. After the first Stefano died, she had Maria Rosa, Irena, and me. Three girls in a row. And then finally she had you. Seven years after the first Stefano died, she had you. So don't be mad at Mamma when she calls you Rosso. That's a sweet name she gives you, with love, because of your red hair. She waited a long time for you. She loves all her boys very much."

———————————

It is late spring. The time of hunger. The winter stores from last year's harvest are now wrinkled old potatoes and shriveled corn, and supplies are running low. The dried pears and plums, specially prepared for the winter months, and the last of the root vegetables are almost gone. Those that remain are hard and withered. It is too soon to pick new crops. When the beans and spring peas come in, we can have a nice minestrone for supper. But now, even the meager handfuls of rice left from last year in the big burlap bag have a stale smell.

I can see my neighbor's chickens bobbing their heads as they roam behind his house, and I think about how nice chickens smell when they're roasted, rubbed with wild rosemary the way my mother makes it. The polenta is not so bad when you can moisten it with a little chicken fat from the pan.

My mamma boils the cornmeal every day to make a porridge and lets it harden into a thick cake. She slices it with a sewing thread, and we grab the slices straight from the cutting board. Sometimes we can season it with some warm pork fat, which my mother saves from the last feast days and heats in a pan. I like looking for little pork cracklings to scoop up with the polenta. But meat is for *sagra*—holy days, like San Rocco's feast day in August, when my mamma puts meat on the table to impress the neighbors. That is a long way off.

My sister bends over the village fountain and fills three buckets of water, two for her and a smaller one for me. She is twelve, just two years older than me, but her back is as strong and straight as a man's. She places the wooden *basul* on her shoulders—she looks like an ox in its yoke—and bends down to hang a full pail on each end. Then she carefully straightens her legs to stand, keeping her balance so as not to lose a drop. But I am small for my age and can barely keep up with her, holding my one little bucket with both hands and trying very hard not to spill it.

On the way back to the house, she stops a minute and puts down her buckets to pull up some young dandelion greens—*tarassacco*—and wild rosemary growing in the fields along the road. The dandelions have to be picked before they flower, although I like their bright yellow blossoms. The greens are a beautiful color this time of year and grow tall in the shade. She also finds some early spring nettles—*ortiche*—pushing their way up through dead leaves. Mamma can use them fresh or dried to make risotto or soups or to cook with spring onions.

She stuffs the greens into the deep pocket in front of her apron. "The greens give some flavor to the polenta," she says, "and the dandelions make a nice salad."

But I don't like to eat dandelions. The taste is too bitter. Even in my hunger, I can be fussy sometimes.

Back at the house, I set the water bucket down where my mamma tells me and quickly run back outside before she can think of something else for me to do. All I can think about is food. I hate going to school hungry, my mind on nothing but my growling stomach instead of my daily lessons.

The town butcher has a house and barn down the road from my family's house, and he has two fat pigs in a little pen outside. Sometimes I see scraps of food in the pig trough that look good enough for me to eat. Today I sneak up quietly, so I don't disturb the pigs and make them squeal. I am in luck. I see a crust of moldy bread in the trough. Quietly, quietly, I tiptoe up to the trough and grab the dry bread. I tuck it inside my shirt and run, fast and sly as a fox, to my favorite hiding place behind the church.

There, I pull out the bread and scrape it against the rough rock foundation of the church, grinding the mold away. As soon as I see the white bread under the mold, I sink my teeth into it. It is cold and hard and smells like the garbage in the pigsty, but I close my eyes and imagine it warm from the bakery oven, smelling sweet and yeasty.

Now, with a few crumbs in my belly, I must rush to school where I will sit and fidget and learn about useless things that will never put food in my mouth.

When the teacher lets us go home for lunch, I decide to stop on the way to see my friend Pino and play with his white donkey, Bianca. Sometimes I find pieces of uneaten carrots or half-chewed apples in the donkey's stable, and I eat those, too, if no one is looking. Once I even tasted the donkey's straw, just to see why the donkey ate it so eagerly, but it had no taste. It was too hard to eat. You must chew and chew on it a long time or else the sharp, pointy bits will cut your mouth.

I don't see the white donkey anywhere as I approach Pino's barn, and look inside. I looked out across the field, and I spot Pino by the edge of the woods, picking up dry branches and twigs for kindling. I run to him to ask where the donkey is.

Pino turns to me with a long face. "Bianca is gone. She got sick. Very sick. A man from Pellegrino Parmense, some kind of doctor, told my father, 'This donkey has tetanus. It has to be killed right away, or it will make all the other animals sick, too.' So my father had to kill Bianca."

I can't believe what Pino is telling me. The pretty donkey was not very old. I don't know what tetanus is, but I am afraid to ask Pino a lot of questions. I think it makes him sad to talk about it.

He tells me one more thing. He says he watched his father beat the poor donkey on the head to kill it. It let out a horrible wail before it died, like the sound of a baby crying.

"It didn't want to die, Rosso! It didn't do anything wrong. It didn't hurt anybody." I can hear in his voice my friend is crying, but he turns away and tries to hide his face from me. Bianca was like a friend to him.

"They buried him, Rosso. Over there in the woods. Your father helped, and your brother. Your Uncle Cesare, too. They dragged him onto the cart and pulled it to the edge of the woods last night. I didn't want to see anymore. I didn't watch."

"I'm sorry, Pino." I don't know what else to say. We sit together for a while under one of the downy oaks, not saying a word. He silently offers me the hard-boiled egg and bread his mother had packed in a kerchief for his lunch. He doesn't want any of it, but I gobble it down. Before long, it is time to go back to school.

As I walk home later that day, I can see smoke rising from the chimney. My mother must be cooking, I think. But there is something else—a smell, like roasting chicken or maybe pork. Or rabbit. Or wild boar. Is it possible? Am I imagining that delicious smell?

My papà appears in the doorway and greets me like an old friend he hasn't seen in a long time.

"Rosso, my boy, come, come!" His arms wrap around me like great eagle wings, caressing me like a baby. "Tonight, we eat, my skinny little boy. We eat!"

I have to go inside and see for myself. My mother's face is red and shining with sweat as she leans over the hot fireplace. She is stirring fatty chunks of meat that are sizzling and spluttering in a big iron pot that hangs on a hook over the fire. The polenta is already sliced and waiting on the table. Giuditta is dressing the dandelion greens in a bowl and drizzles them with a few precious drops of olive oil—the kind we usually save for *sagra*.

The table is set with five plates for my mamma and papà, my brother Pietro, Giuditta, and me. I'm the baby, so the smallest plate is always for me. *Someday*, I think to myself, *I'll be a papà with a house full of children, and I'll get the biggest plate*. I'll be the king of the house. I will have a big house and lots of money, my children will be fat and happy, and I will do nothing but eat and drink all day long.

After this unexpected feast, while my mother and sister wash the dishes and pans, I sit at the table with my father and brother and rest my hands on my full belly. I can't remember the last time I ate so well. Uncle Cesare stops by, his accordion under his arm, and greets my father with a warm embrace and a full hearty laugh.

"*Ciao*, Bartò! How you feel, *fratellino*? You still hungry, eh? Ha ha!" He pulls up a chair next to my papà.

My Uncle Cesare looks like my papà's twin, both with thick moustaches the color of salt and pepper. Both are laughing, and I don't know why they are in such high spirits. My big brother Pietro leans back in his chair and picks his teeth with a bit of straw. He is fifteen years older than me, dark and sharp-featured with deep-set brooding eyes. He is eyeing me with a grin on his face.

"Tell me, Rosso," Pietro asks. "Did you like your supper tonight?"

"I did! It was the best rabbit stew I ever had!"

At this, the room explodes in laughter. The men are slapping their knees. My mamma is trying to hold back, clenching her mouth, but bellies are shaking with laughter and eyes are glistening with tears.

"That was no rabbit! But it had long ears like a rabbit!" my papà says, mimicking the shape of ears with his hands behind his head and baring his two front teeth, prancing around the room and braying like a fool. At this, the room shakes with a second wave of laughter, men stomping their feet and clutching their ribs as if they are trying to stop themselves from bursting.

Pietro leans over and says softly in my ear, "Don't tell anyone, Rosso, but last night, while you were sleeping, some of us went out in the woods and dug up Pino's donkey. Dug him right out of the hole where we buried him just a few hours before. We chopped him up and shared the meat."

I look at my brother's face—I can tell he's not joking.

"Bianca? You chopped up Bianca? We had Bianca for supper?"

"When an animal is dead, it has no name. It is only meat."

"But I loved Bianca! And she was sick, Pietro. Won't we get sick, too?"

"What do you want, Rosso? You die of hunger, or you die from eating a sick animal. Which do you prefer?"

Pietro's eyes are locked on mine. I don't have an answer.

Now Uncle Cesare is starting up on his accordion, my father is singing with his full voice, and my mother's hips are swaying as she scrubs her cutting board clean. My papà is the happiest I have ever seen him, a strong solid man in his sixties, his eyes twinkling like a child's.

Maria Rosa, 1880

Oh, take me up there! I can love you
In the face of the biting mountain breezes,
Among cyclamens and firs, and intoxicate you
With morning smiles and caresses!

Here gray fog lingers on my heart;
Poetry dies in the rice fields;
I want to love you up there, in the mountains
In the immortal silence. Take me away!

—*Ada Negri, from "Take Me Away"*

Look at him. Mr. Big Shot. Standing on his little horse-drawn cart, like a little Julius Caesar on his chariot, so full of himself. I watch him from the corner of my eyes. The horse pulls him through the rice paddies so he doesn't get his delicate feet wet, while we, the *mondine*, stand barefoot in the mud, water up to our knees, bent over from the waist, the sun beating down its misery on our backs.

In these watery plains of Pavia, we stand in rows, thousands of women, like the women who have done for generations before us. They say Italy grows all the rice that is served across Europe, for all those bowls of risotto that people eat with such pleasure, with their porcini, their chestnuts, their wild boar, in all the great cities to the north.

The people who know things, people of the world, they tell me this. But no one knows about me. I am just another poor *mondina*.

"Don't look up," Luigia says. "The *caporalo* is coming this way."

"I know. I see him. He has eyes for you, not for me."

Our Good Name

The nerve of that man. The big *capu di risi*. He drives up in his little cart close to where we are working, pulls the reins of his horse to stop, and stares down at Luigia's bare white legs. Her long skirt is drawn up between her thighs and tucked inside her belt like a loose diaper.

"You there, with the striped skirt. Stop. Stand up. Come closer."

I try to pretend I don't see him and keep my head down, working the row. What filthy thing does he have on his mind? Then he leans over from his cart and pulls a leech from Luigia's thigh and drops it into a little clay jar.

Luigia stands motionless, too frightened to speak, as a trickle of blood runs down her leg.

"Back to work, you foolish cow!" The *capu* then proceeds down the line of bent-over women, staring at their legs as he rides past.

"What was that all about?" I ask my friend.

"The *caporali* go up and down and collect the leeches from our bodies and sell them to the pharmacy. They make good money from them."

"*Managgia alla miseria.* It's not enough that they take a cut of our pay—for doing nothing—but now they have to make money off our blood, too?"

The leeches seem to stay away from me. I wear thick woolen stockings that go all the way up to my thighs. My mother knit them specially for me to keep the mosquitoes off my legs and to keep the frogs and snakes from nibbling at my ankles.

———————

Ever since I was fourteen, I have worked the rice fields of Pavia, more than one hundred kilometers from my home in Pereto. Sometimes the village girls went to Vercelli or Novara, but I always came to Pavia. Late April, that was always the time of sadness and pain. That was the time I had to leave my mamma and my dear family to go and work for a little money and a bag of rice. I came by oxcart and then by train, and then by oxcart again. Forty days away from my family.

They say there are more than a hundred thousand of us women and girls who come to the fields every spring like hungry migrating birds. Only women can do this work, they say. Our delicate hands are needed to plant the tender rice shoots and then tend them daily, pulling the little weeds around them. Such precious things, these tiny rice plants that demand constant care, whose lives are more important than ours—we, the worthless migrant women who slave over them all day.

We start working one hour before dawn and finish one hour after sunset. Breaking our backs all day, with the *caporali* grinning at us like hungry wolves, men who stand by in comfort with sticks in their hands, ready to beat us without needing an excuse. They stare at us, with our *culi* in the air, our bare legs. If we dare to stand up to give our backs a rest, they come at us with their long sticks to beat us back down again.

Sometimes when the *caporali* aren't looking, I stop to straighten my back and look beyond the flooded plains to see the Alps to the north and the Apennines to the south. Somewhere over the mighty Alps, whose snowcaps pierce the clouds, lies the whole world. Cities with names like Paris and London. Everything that is fine and easy in the world behind those mountains. But I long for the green Apennines to the south. The place I call home. And the man who loves me, who roots me like a kernel of corn that takes hold in the ground.

We sleep at night in a barn, a place not fit for animals. If you are lucky, you get a spot inside. If you arrive too late, there is only room under the overhang outside. Sleeping is no comfort with mosquitos buzzing in our ears, barely enough beans and rice to fill our bellies, a little bit of hay for a mattress, and the cold earth below. Nothing can block the buzzing, buzzing, all day and all night, buzzing even in my dreams.

Finally, it is June, and I am on my way home. My work is done. I am proud to have a little money in my pocket to give to my family and a sack of dry rice from last year's harvest in my bag. I can feel the air grow cool as the oxcart draws nearer to my mountain home, in the air the smell of downy oaks in late spring. I love the crunch of wooden wheels over acorns and stony paths. Everything is green.

As we make the turn around the Oratorio di San Rocco, the stone chapel where Metti ends and the *frazione* of Pereto begins, I can see men in the corn fields bending over the rows of young plants, breaking up the weeds with their hoes. I look for a young man wearing a familiar billowing white shirt and a straw hat with a long pheasant feather in it.

One man in the cornfield stops his work when he sees the oxcart draw near, leans for a moment on his hoe, and then lets it drop to the ground. He is running down the narrow rows between the corn. Running to me.

"Maria Rosa!" he yells, waving his straw hat in the air.

I beg the driver to stop the cart and hand him his fare. By now, the young man is at the cart, reaching up to help me down.

"Antò!"

The driver climbs down from the cart and lays my bag by the road while Antonio wraps his arms around me. His shirt is wet from the sweat of his labors. I love the earthy smell of his body. It is the first time I have felt like a woman and not like a beast of burden in many long weeks.

"Look at you, Maria Rosa. Brown as a chestnut, and all bones. Didn't they feed you? Look—I can wrap my hands around your little waist, my fingertips touching front and back."

"You missed me, Antò?"

I look away, conscious of my dusty appearance, trying to re-arrange my tousled hair as he looks at me. He is the most beautiful young man in the village, and he is smiling at me with his whole face.

"Let me go home now, wash away the dust of my travels. You will come to the house later?"

"I will be there, my angel." He kisses me hard on the mouth with a great smacking sound before letting me go.

In the evening after supper, I pace the floor, waiting for Antonio to arrive. I am wearing a clean white blouse and a new blue skirt my mother had sewn for me. I had to take in the waist and cinch it with a cloth sash. I have lost so much weight during my forty days in the rice fields. Men like a little flesh on a woman, but I feel like a broomstick.

Antonio arrives with his mother, father, and sisters, and my papà pours little glasses of his homemade wine to celebrate my return. It is a special occasion to have the whole family home together.

In the fall, it will be the men's turn to go and do the heavy work of harvesting the rice. Antonio, too. They will cut the rice plants with their sickles—back-breaking work—and carry the sheaves to a place where they will be laid out to dry for a few days. Then the men will bang the plants against the wooden thresher to free the rice from the stalks.

So much human misery for a single grain of rice.

———————

Antonio and I sit together on the wooden chest by the fireplace. I'd like to go outside with him, just the two of us, and see his face in the moonlight, but we are not allowed to go anywhere without a chaperone. And so we sit inside, as close to each other as possible without provoking my mother's frown.

"I don't want to wait, Marì," he whispers in my ear. "We could get married, now, before I go away to the rice harvest."

"Antò, you know I want to. But why the rush? You'll have a little more money after the harvest."

"I care nothing about the money, and we don't need a big wedding."

"Tell that to my mother. Her first daughter to get married? She will want to impress everyone in town with a wedding feast, even if she has to beg and borrow the money."

"We don't have to tell anyone. We can run away to another town. Another country even. I don't want to go to the harvest this year."

"It's just a few months away, and you'll be home before you know."

"I want you as my bride before I go. If I have to sweat all day in the sun and lie awake at night with aches in my back, for many long weeks, I want the thought of you and our wedding night to soothe me to my sleep."

"We should wait, Antò. My mother would never forgive me."

"I don't want to leave you. Not this year. In my heart, I know I should stay. I belong here with you."

I don't understand the strange sadness in his eyes. I want him to be glad for my return. To feel hope and happiness about our future life together. I give him a gentle smile, but it does nothing to soften the darkness in his eyes.

———————————

The day has come when Antonio has to go *ai risaie*. He and all the other men of the village clamber onto the oxcarts with their meager personal belongings rolled up in their blankets to head north for the rice harvest. I have come to see him off, giving him the extra bread and cheese that I've saved for his journey.

"I'll be back soon, Maria Rosa, to marry you. I promise. You stay true to me."

"How can I not be true to you? You are taking all the young men in the village with you!"

That makes him laugh a little, and it helps me hide the sadness I feel. It is good to see some lightness in his face as he waves goodbye. I watch him until his cart disappears around the bend in the road.

Only two weeks have gone by when a rumor arrives in our village, passed from person to person. The rumor is carried on the lips of a young boy who bursts into my house as my mother and I are grinding corn: Antonio is coming home early.

But so soon? He has only been gone a couple weeks. Did he leave his job to come home to me? Did he run away? Is he so eager to marry me? Or is he in some kind of trouble?

I untie my apron, drape it over a chair, and walk out of the house, repeating the words in my head: *So soon? So soon? Did he lose his job? Did he do something foolish?*

I walk at a fast clip, seeing nothing but the road ahead of me, moving with a single-minded purpose toward the main mountain road that leads north from the village. I feel nothing, not even the sharp pebbles under my thin shoes. The fields disappear and drop away on either side of me. If someone called out to me, I would not know. I hear nothing.

I walk until I see the mule approach, pulling the oxcart behind it. Two young men are sitting up front, one older, one younger. As they draw near, I think one of them is Antonio. But it is not him. It only looks like him. It is his younger brother Raffaello.

I run toward the cart.

"Raffaello! Where is Antonio?"

Raffaello jumps from the cart to stop me. "Don't look, Maria."

The cargo on the cart. The blanket that looks like Antonio's. The blanket covering the box. The box that is a coffin. The coffin that contains… No one. Nothing.

"I tried to tell him, Maria. He was cutting the rice. He cut his hand with the sickle. A bad cut. It was infected, smelled bad. He told no one. Afraid they would send him home. He wanted to work. He wanted the money. For your wedding."

Raffaello's hands are reaching forward to me, as if beseeching me to understand. I turn my back to him and walk home. There is nothing inside me to say.

I am silent that day, and for all the days to come. I walk in and out of days and weeks and months as if they are an endless row of vacant rooms.

It will be six more years of moving through the world this way, alone and mute, before the day comes when I will end my long silence. And that's when I marry Raffaello.

Stefano, 1882

My family always had sheep, as far back as anyone can remember. Always just two or three, maybe a lamb. They were never to sell, but to give us wool. My mother and sisters knit sweaters, *le maglie*. They call my family *Marenghi Maglie* because we are the Marenghis that make sweaters. There are other Marenghi families in the *frazioni* of Metti, Pereto, Bore, and Casale, not related to us, and we tell ourselves apart with these special names. Some are stonemasons, some butchers. We are the Marenghis who have sheep and make sweaters. *Marenghi Maglie.*

My mamma, Elisabetta Resmini—her friends call her Bettina—taught my sisters how to knit, crochet, and even make delicate lace with a tatting needle. They weave sweaters, blankets, shawls, socks, hats, and scarves. Most of these are for us, the family, to keep us warm, but sometimes they trade a sweater or some yarn for eggs or cheese or a little olive oil. I never have a coat in the winter—just a lot of sweaters, one worn over the other. I don't like the itchy feel of the wool on my neck, but I know better than to complain.

One afternoon in early December, my sisters Maria Rosa and Giuditta are knitting by the fire. Outside, an early snow is falling, so it is a day for indoor work. My mother is mashing boiled potatoes by crushing them with her hands on the breadboard. She is making a potato pie— *torta di patate.*

"Where's Papà today?" I ask.

"He is with Pietro and your *Zio* Cesare, stacking hay in the Salvi barn," she says, never looking up from her cooking. She mixes the potatoes with some reserved pork fat, a little cheese, and some herbs before pressing the mixture into a large rectangular pan that she has already prepared with a thin flour-and-water crust. "They'll come home hungry tonight, that's for sure."

"Can I go play with little Angelina?"

"You mean the lamb? Don't be giving names to animals. Then you won't want to part with them when the time comes."

"But she looks like an *Angelina*. A little angel, so soft and white. She has big, sweet eyes and a little pink nose…"

"Don't talk about an animal that way!"

"But Mamma, we're not going eat Angelina, are we?"

"No, she is not for us to eat. We keep the lamb just in case. She's like money in the bank. Somebody gets sick or breaks a bone, that lamb is like gold. She is how we pay the doctor if we need one and don't have money."

"But then the doctor will eat Angelina?"

Losing her patience, she shouts, "He can wear the lamb like a hat on his head if he wants to!"

"But Mamma…"

"*Uffa!* You're too tender-hearted, Rosso. Too delicate, like a girl. You're twelve years old now. You need to be strong, thick-skinned, like a man."

Giuditta looks up from her knitting, gives me her usual sympathetic look, then turns to Mamma with the wide beseeching eyes of a beggar asking for bread.

"What, you too?" Mamma shakes her head at Giuditta. "I don't know why I have so many children. All soft in the head. I wish I only had one, two, maybe three—*e basta così!* Maybe then you have enough for everyone to eat. But I had to have nine children. Nine. And what do I get for all my trouble? *La miseria.*"

My mother's disappointment with her life hangs like a heavy shroud over the room. Everyone is quiet now and afraid to speak. There is nothing to say when Mamma gets in one of her black moods.

I quietly start to slip out of the room.

"Where you going?"

"I'm going to check the sheep, make sure they have hay, Mamma."

"You clean the stable, Rosso. Clean it good. And make sure their water is not ice. Break the ice with a stick so they can eat the ice."

I wrap myself in my sweaters and scratchy hat and head for the stable. Little Angelina jumps and hops when she sees me. She is six months old, still a spring lamb in my mind, her hair curled like little question marks all over her body. She thinks I am playing a game when I sweep the manure out of the stalls and then use the pitchfork to tease out fresh hay for the sheep. She hops around me as I work. I always think Angelina is smiling at me.

My Angelina. How could anyone not see what an angel she is? I remember how her legs looked when she was younger. They looked like they were too long for her, like the legs of a wobbly table. Now she has a little more fat on her, but she still stands on her long baby legs.

I pick her up and hold her to my chest like a *bambina*, wrapping my sweaters around her, keeping us both warm.

"I won't let anyone take you away, my Angelina. You're my little angel. No one's going to make a meal out of you."

I step out into the snow that falls as light as pinfeathers. Holding Angelina in my arms, I dance, I twirl. Little Angelina is my dance partner. I sing her a soft lullaby, *Ninna Nanna, Ninna Nanna,* as the sky turns a soft pearl gray and the light fades. I waltz down the road, spinning until I am dizzy, singing softly, the snowflakes sticking to my sweater and to Angelina's soft curly head.

We come to the old wooden bridge that crosses over the ravine. Its wooden planks are slick with the newly fallen wet snow.

"Get ready to slide! Hold on tight!"

I make a running start, and we glide over the slippery bridge. I try to turn the forward slide into a graceful spin, but that's when I lose control and slam hard against the handrailing. The startled lamb goes flying from my arms and over the handrails, tumbling down into the rocky depths below.

"No! No! Angelina!"

My scream echoes as I lean over the rail and look down into the deep ravine. In this fading light, I can barely make out the white lamb lying motionless on the snow-covered rocks. I think she may have broken her neck.

My heart is pounding. I want to wail out in sorrow, but I have to calm myself. It is too dangerous to climb down the ravine, the rocks slippery with snow and ice. I must go back to the house and say nothing. I know nothing. I will let everyone think the lamb got away by herself. I don't want to get into any trouble.

Mamma will never forgive me. Ever! I lost her precious lamb, her money in the bank. I wipe my tears on my sleeve, stiffen my back, and hope no one will notice the pain written on my face.

The snow is starting to thicken, with large puffy flakes, and the light in the sky is growing dimmer. As I approach the house, I can see the outlines of three men down the road, looking like black ghosts against the white landscape. As they get closer, I can see that the one in the middle is limp and dragging his feet, like a wounded soldier, and the ones on either side are holding him up at the shoulders. One of them is shouting, "*Bettina! Bettina!*"

My mamma throws open the door. In the light from the house, I can see my brother Pietro and *Zio* Cesare are holding up my father, his head slumped downward. My mother is screaming, "*Bartò! Barto!*" as the men guide him into the house.

I am still swallowing the pain of losing my sweet little lamb, but now a new pain is layered like a knit shawl over the other. I run into the house, yelling, "*Papà!*"

The men lay my father out on the bed and loosen his scarf and sweaters. My father looks like a man who is sleeping peacefully.

"What happened? Tell me!" Mamma demands.

"We are working, like always," Pietro said. "Then Papà says he doesn't feel so good. He says his neck hurts, then his arm. He doesn't feel his arm. He looks shaky, weak. His legs give out and he falls down, says he can't breathe."

"*Il cuore!* It's his heart, just like his father. His heart! Rosso, you run and get the doctor. Tell him your papà needs him right away. Tell him we got a nice lamb for him. We can pay him."

I stare at her, frozen with fear and shame.

"*Vai! Vai!* Go now! Don't stand there like a fool. And get Father Lazaro, too!"

I do as my mamma tells me. I run and get the doctor first, and then I run to the church for Father Lazaro. When the priest and I arrive at the house together, everyone is crying.

Father Lazaro says a prayer over my father, but I think he knows it is too late for the last rites. He doesn't want my mother to know my father's soul has already slipped away before he can give his blessing. The doctor consoles my mother, puts his arms around her shoulders, tells her not to cry, not to worry. He promises he'll come back in the morning and help her make all the arrangements.

My mother sits on the bed beside my father, holding his hand with both of hers, making shrill mournful sounds like a wounded animal. I have never heard such sounds. *Zio* Cesare sits on the other side of the bed, holding his brother's other hand. Everyone else—Pietro, Maria Rosa, Giuditta, and I— gather around the kitchen table, heads down, holding handkerchiefs over our mouths to muffle our sobs. Only Pietro is silent, his eyes wet but his features hard as stone.

Mamma's potato pie is sitting on the cupboard shelf, still steaming, wrapped in a towel. No one is hungry.

Pietro quietly steps out into the bracing winter night. I follow close behind, shuddering, and stand beside him as he leans against the house, hands in his pockets. Puffs of frozen breath float and drift around our heads.

"Pietro, what happens now?"

"We do what we have to do. We go to church tomorrow, give our papà a funeral, pay our respects, say our goodbyes. We help our mother. That's what men do. She needs our help more than ever. We work. We keep going. Like always."

"So you'll stay? You won't go away and get married? If you do, then I'll have to be the man of the house. I'm too young to be the man of the house!"

Pietro's expression softens as looks tenderly down at me. "Don't worry about that, Rosso. I can't go anywhere now."

"But you want to leave, don't you? You're twenty-seven. You're going to be an old man soon. What about Amalia? What if she won't wait for you?"

"Who told you about Amalia? Never mind that. It's not the time to think of such things. Go to bed, Rosso. Go kiss your mother and go to bed."

I leave Pietro standing alone in the night. I slouch back into the house and tiptoe up to my mother to kiss her cheek. Then I crawl onto the lumpy mattress I share with Pietro, trying to smooth out the *scartossi* under the canvas cover to make the mattress softer. I pull the knit blankets up to my chin and think about Angelina, my poor tiny lamb, cold and broken and dying all alone at the bottom of a ravine.

And I think about my father, who never listened to my mamma when she said he was too old to do heavy work. Now he is lying flat on his back, like a tree knocked down by a winter ice storm. He is sixty-nine years old.

Pietro, 1884

Like the great martyr of Rome, my name means "stone." Just as Saint Peter was the rock of Christ, I am Pietro, the rock of my family.

Or so my mother likes to remind me. Constantly.

When my father died two years ago, I became the man of the family. I inherited my father's masonry tools, his mallet, chisels, and straight edge, along with the tools he used to work the soil. For him, knowing how to chisel stone was just something a man does, along with sowing corn, shearing sheep, and building heavy wooden furniture for his home. Like many poor villagers, he did not have just one trade but many. There was no other choice.

I was determined that I would be different. I would be a master stone-mason. I would take the stone that is mined from the earth and bend it to my will. I would build a good life for my future children, better than the one that I knew, and I would build it stone by stone.

I marry my darling Amalia on February 20, 1884. I wish my father could have lived to see the day. My poor little brother Stefano, just fourteen years old, is crying more than anyone. He is too soft-hearted, that one. I tell Stefano he will have to be a man now and look after his mother and two sisters. But that is not completely true. I am not going very far. I have built a new stone house for Amalia directly across the road from my mother's house. I will help Stefano take care of our mother and sisters for many more years to come.

Our first son is born almost a year to the day from my wedding day, but to our great sorrow, he is born dead. This anguish is nothing like the grief that I felt for my father, who lived to see almost seventy years. That is the proper span of a man's life, as the Bible tells us. But this tender baby boy, my own flesh, who looks so perfect and calm, as if he is merely sleeping in Amalia's arms, never even shared with us his first cry.

I take the baby from my wife and hold him in my arms. Drawing back the blanket to see his wrinkled face, I ask, "What, you have nothing to say to me? We wait for you all this time, and you have nothing to say?"

Our next four children are all girls: Carolina, Albina, Maria Rosa, and Tranquilla. I will have a house full of girls, and it seems they are no less hungry than little boys. But if I have only girls, I will have no one to learn my trade, no one to inherit my house and animals and my workshop full of fine stone-working tools.

Every morning, I leave my house before the girls are awake, and with nothing in my stomach, I walk to the neighboring villages: Franchi, Ferrari, Bore, and Ralli. I descend mountain paths with heavy tools on my back, crossing streams, then climbing up the steep slopes on the other side. I go wherever my work is needed, and I eat nothing until I return to my house at night with aching feet and blistered hands. But I am better off than most. I have earned a reputation that is more valuable than my house and land and everything on it. People send for me when they need a strong stone house or stable or a wall that can withstand occasional tremors in the earth.

From the time I was married, I began to notice that the men I knew, the ones who worked in stone alongside me, were starting to disappear. One by one, they were abandoning their Apennine villages and migrating to the New World. Some go to Canada, some to Argentina, but most of them were leaving for America.

In some ways, this improves my own circumstances. There is less competition for my work, and my skills are even more valued. I can charge a little more money. But with so many men leaving, the women are left to work the farms and tend to the livestock. It is getting harder for the women to pay for anything with their husbands far away, and they can only barter what little they have in return for my labors.

Sometimes the women pay me with the bread they bake, or potato pie, or clothes they sew for my girls. Some of them raise silkworms in their houses, and they pay for my work with spools of coarse silk thread. Others are *mondine*, like my sister, who work for a few coins and sacks of rice in the northern rice fields. They offer me rice in exchange for mending a stone wall or building a fireplace.

These meager exchanges, I fear, will never be enough to feed my growing family. I start to think that maybe I should go to America, too. When my poor mother died in 1889, just six years after my father's passing, I began to feel more heavily the weight of my family's destiny on my shoulders. It will be up to me and my brother Stefano to maintain our shared land with its two houses and a stable and to ensure there will be a male heir to carry on our good name.

When Stefano turned fourteen, he became my apprentice. We often talk about building our fortunes together and how one day he will have a family of his own. We hope to raise our families side by side. But until we can get more payment for our work, our earnings will not feed one family, let alone two.

In 1894, while Amalia is carrying Tranquilla in her belly, I begin to talk to Stefano about going to America. Our sister Maria Rosa has already married, and Giuditta is engaged to Giuseppe Cornoni; they are talking about America, too. Soon, Stefano will be alone in the family house, a young man in his early twenties, and he has little to offer a prospective bride. As the younger brother, he will inherit nothing.

The house where he and my sister live is already showing signs of neglect. The roof is sagging in the middle like the back of an old mare. It looks as if it is about to collapse. The gardens around the house grow wild and weedy since Stefano and I aren't there to help tend them. We are spending our daylight hours repairing walls and houses for others, often several villages away from our home. There is no time to tend to our own homes.

A few of the men from the villages of Metti and Pereto have gone to a place that is impossible to pronounce—Mass-a-chu-setts. There are stories I hear of granite quarries, rich with a rare spotted stone that has a rosy-pink color when it is polished. There are also rumors of many factories beside a great river, factories that make everything from powerful machines to ladies' shoes and straw hats, and there are good-paying jobs for any man with a strong back and a will to work. Any man who goes there will soon have pockets full of gold and grand homes that look like castles, living out their days in a land of peace and plenty. That's what I hear. I want to go and see this fabled place for myself.

There is talk of a man named Giacomo Cenedella. He comes from a village called Lonato del Gardo in the Brescia province, near Lake Garda. He is a *padrone*, someone who recruits strong young men to work in the quarries and factories of his American town. He knows Father Lazaro, the priest at San Leonardo Abate, the church in Metti where everyone from all the neighboring villages goes to be baptized or married. I persuade Stefano to go with me and talk with Father Lazaro.

"Father Lazaro," I say, "we hear talk about the man from Lake Garda who is looking for strong men to come to America for work."

"Ah, *il padrone*. Yes, I know of him. Already he has recruited hundreds of men from these mountains. All of them seem destined to go to a place called Massachusetts."

"But what are these jobs?"

"There is work in the stone quarries, hard work. But men of your skills, as stonemasons, may find a place there. Mostly, they are looking for men to work the factories. There are iron workers, shoemakers, cigar makers—many types of work. And there is work building roads, bridges, and farm work, too."

"How do men pay for the voyage?"

"The steamship costs very little, if you travel third-class. If you need help paying your fare, the *padrone* can arrange for your travel, and the cost will come out of your pay every month once you start working in America. Cenedella speaks English, and his job is to be the middle-man between you and the company you work for."

"Then that is easy! We can do that. Do you think this *padrone* would be interested in my brother and me?"

"Oh, Pietro, I have to speak what is in my heart. I hope you will not go. You have a family, a house full of children already, and you are well respected here. We have already lost so many men, but you—please, not you, Pietro. You belong here, with us. We need you here.

"Stefano, you are a different story. You have no family yet. The *padrones*, they prefer unmarried men with no attachments to distract them from their work and tug their hearts back to Italy. You would be of interest to them. Yes, I see that now. And later, after you make a little money, maybe you can come back home to our little village, too?"

"Yes, Father, I want to go," Stefano says. "Every year the food here is more scarce with fewer men to work the soil. There is nothing but corn on our tables most of the year, thin watered-down polenta, with maybe a few bitter greens to change the flavor. My sister, Maria Rosa, already suffers from the *pellagra.* She wears the red rash around her neck like a collar."

"Yes, yes, I know. It is from eating only corn. You need more money to buy better food. You can make good money in America. Send some back to your family. It's a good plan. And so, you wish to go then?"

"Only if Pietro comes, too. I won't go without my brother."

"And I don't want my brother to go alone, either," I say. "We will go together."

"But Pietro, isn't Amalia with child?"

"Yes. I will wait until the child arrives in the new year, and then we will go. Amalia will not be alone. She will have my sister Giuditta to help her while we are away. We have to go and see this place called America. We must do this for our family."

Father Lazaro agrees to write to *il Signor* Cenedella, and from that moment on, I can think of nothing but America. Stefano is a little anxious at first, but little by little, I can see his excitement grow. He has come to understand, through my constant reminders and coaxing, that he will have very little to look forward to here in our little *frazione* of Pereto, our parents gone, living in his older brother's shadow with nothing to bequeath to his sons.

In America, I tell him, he can be a man of importance.

On January 18, 1895, the midwife delivers our fourth child. I wait outside the door to my bedroom, pacing the floor, while Carolina tries patiently to corral her little sisters Albina and Maria Rosa. Finally, I hear our baby's loud complaint, its first little roar against the world, and my three daughters are all startled into stillness. I go to my wife, who is sitting up in bed, while the midwife washes the wailing child in a basin.

"*Stai calma! Tranquilla!*" the midwife coos gently at the baby. I know instantly by the little feminine vowel at the end of *tranquilla* that I have another girl. Amalia stares at me with probing eyes.

"Shall we call her Tranquilla, my darling?" I hoped that little joke would draw a smile from her.

"You wanted a son, Pietro, I know. Maybe if I gave you a son, you would stay here with me and not go to America."

"No, Amalia, no. I need to go and see if there is something in this New Country that I can give to you and my children. If there is a better life for us, I need to know."

"You will never come back. You won't."

"I will, my love. I promise. You know I don't want to leave you. I have no choice. Already half the men are gone from our village. When there is only half enough food to feed us, half of us must go."

"But you can't swim! You will be lost at sea and drown! Or you will find a pretty young American girl who will bewitch you. She will put a spell on you! And I will be left here alone with my girls without anyone to protect us!"

"No, Amalia. I will never leave you. I promise. Giuditta will be here to help you until I return. I *will* return. And your next child will be a son, and the one after that. You'll see."

Pietro, 1895

We have walked so long
Our home has narrowed
To the width of our shoes.

*—From the poem "The Refugee
Considers the Faucet," by Philip Metres*

The news of our decision to emigrate to America soon spreads from mouth to ear to mouth to ear, finding its way to every house in Pereto and the neighboring villages. Two other men want to join us. One, Giulio Franchi, is the same age as Stefano, and the other, Domenico Salvi, is close to my age. We decide to sail together. We agree to leave in the spring, when the weather will be better for travel, and by then, we will have earned a few more *soldi* to have in our pockets for the journey.

The families of those who have gone before say that the easiest way to America is from France. We hear that the ships from Italy—mostly out of Napoli and Genova—are filthy and overcrowded, with men packed together like rats. The other way is to take the train north, over the Alps and across France, arriving at last in the port of Le Havre, Normandy, on the northwest coast. Many of my Northern Italian countrymen choose this route to the New World. It seems like a long way to go to board a ship, but others have done it before us. And we trust the word of our *padrone.*

Stefano seems full of lightness and bright expectations. He is twenty-five, but I know my brother. He is really just a child. He has never traveled anywhere. He went from his mother's womb to the slightly bigger womb of our little village. He is still waiting to be born.

As for me, I may not have traveled far, but I have seen a little of the world. I was once a rice worker, up in the northern plains of Pavia, so I know something of dusty roads, oxcarts, and trains. I know what it is to sleep in a place that is not my home.

One time, instead of coming home after the rice harvest, I ventured a little further north. I took the train from Pavia to Milano, and I came home by way of Parma. It meant spending some of my precious earnings, but I had to see at least one of the great cities of the world. I had no money for lodging—I slept only on trains or in churches—and I had very little to spend on food. But at least I could see the Duomo of Milan and the opera house—the magnificent La Scala. Of course, there was no money for opera tickets. The only music I heard was in my mind, imagining the soaring operas of Giuseppe Verdi, whose songs are so catchy, they are remembered and sung by ordinary people in every village in Italy.

Stefano knows nothing of travel. Maybe that's why he grins so hard whenever I say the word *America*. He is amazed by everything I tell him. I told him America was named after one of our countrymen, Amerigo Vespucci, the famous map maker. I tell him about the great explorers, the voyages of Columbus. He must have been taught these things in school, as I was, but he remembers nothing, so all this strikes him as astonishing news.

I am not so lighthearted as my brother. I am propelled to the New World by a sense of duty. I feel it in my bones, a matter of honor and respect for my family. It hardens my resolve. I could never be at peace if I went to my grave not knowing if there was a better life for my family. If there is a place where I can do better as a husband and father, I have to go and see it.

That is not to say I won't miss this place I know so well. These beautiful mountains, these Apennines, that spread like a green paper fan over the smiling face of the sun.

———————

Our Good Name

We leave the first week of May, 1895. Amalia insists once more that I stay. She has a bad feeling. She has had fantastic dreams and wild premonitions of ships sinking and trains crashing. Sometimes she awakes, screaming in the night. I tell her not to worry. Before the corn is harvested this year, I will either send for her and the girls or I will come back to her. I promise her this. I give each of my four little angels a kiss on the head and embrace my wife hard, very hard, so she will understand how much I love her.

When we arrive at the port of Le Havre, we stand in line to give our names to the ship master. I can't imagine so many people fitting on one boat. I tell him my age is forty, but he writes it as fifty—perhaps he sees the weariness on my face from traveling over two days by train and having nowhere to sleep but in our third-class seats.

The ship is called *La Champagne.* That seems like a good joke to me. I can't wait to tell people back at my village how we were transported in luxury across the Atlantic, as if floating in a crystal glass of champagne. People have heard such wild tales of America, of rivers overflowing with milk and honey and fertile fields that grow giant carrots as tall as a man. Some people are inclined to believe anything.

The reality is much different. La Champagne is a black and battered iron vessel with two hulking smoke funnels and four tall masts. There is nothing about it that even suggests champagne. It seems more fitting for transporting cattle than for people. It holds more than a thousand passengers, mostly in third-class. I cannot imagine what first-class passengers receive to make them feel the extra expense is worth it.

We are at sea for three weeks. Between the ocean turbulence and the rancid food, most of us are sick to our stomachs throughout the journey. My intestines are tied up in knots, and I am almost grateful for the agony it brings me. It keeps me from wanting anymore of that slop they pile onto our plates. The sleeping area has a bad smell, a mix of vomit and piss sloshing around in open pails, making any hope of rest or recovery impossible. By the time we arrive at New York harbor, we all have looser clothes and deeper hollows in our cheeks.

After some darkly cold days at sea, the sun starts burning through the cloud cover and a sharp ray of light glints off the torch of the Statue of Liberty, as if someone had lit the flame just for us. Everyone is on deck, pushing toward the front of the boat for a better view, jumping and cheering when the statue appears. Stefano is as giddy as a child about to see his first circus, waving his Alpine hat like a madman, but so are all the others. Grown men are jumping and cheering as if Lady Liberty can hear them. I simply stand and look at the colossal Lady, wondering what she is trying to say to us.

There are very few things I remember from my school days, but I suddenly think back to the fables our teacher used to read to us about Jason and the Argonauts and the sirens that bedeviled them. The female apparitions were thought to be the ravings of sailors driven to madness by the sea. They imagined seeing human forms in the coastal rocks. Some said they were mermaids, with the upper body of a woman and the lower body of a sea bird or a fish with angelic wings attached to their shoulders. Their sweet voices lured the weary travelers to their doom. I wonder now what enticing song Lady Liberty is singing to us and what terrifying animal forms she is concealing underneath her long-pleated robe.

As we dock at our first stop in New York Harbor, we watch the first-class passengers disembark to enter the city directly, while the rest of second- and third-class citizens are carried by ferry to Ellis Island. In this smaller boat, we are closer to the water. It is not the clear sapphire blue I would expect to find around this legendary jeweled city—this place of wealth and power. The water is so opaque; I can see nothing below the surface, just an oily brown skin that stretches like a stain. Our ferry stirs up a brown froth as it plows forward. And the smell! I would not eat any fish from those waters. Do the people of this city empty their garbage into this harbor? Do they dump their dead animals here?

As we pull up to the dock, we are greeted by a grayish wooden structure, a monstrous building, maybe two hundred meters wide, looking more like a prison than a place of welcome.

A few years later, I would learn this ugly barracks had burned down, to be replaced by a grander building of stone. Good riddance, I think. Good riddance.

As we disembark, we are forced into long lines. Men in white coats poke and prod us like animals on our way to slaughter. Will they think I have enough meat on me to pass inspection? Am I fat enough for you to butcher, Mr. Man-in-a-White-Coat?

I see a fellow passenger who had caught a bad cold on the journey. I will never forget the look of panic on his face when they mark his back with the "X" in white chalk. He will be sent on the next ship back home. Finally, we can breathe a long sigh of relief when we pass inspection, and our backs are not branded with an "X."

Hundreds of us are herded onto ferries to Manhattan. Ferries heading to steamships. Steamships heading north along the coast. We have to endure rough waters to go from New York to Stonington, Connecticut, and pick up the train from there. We are loaded from one crowded conveyance to the next, until we find ourselves in a train car bound for Milford, Massachusetts. Someone always seems to know what to do, and the rest of us blindly follow. We are too tired and confused to do otherwise.

I do my best to catch a glimpse of this New Country that we are passing over, craning my neck to see through our train windows. I don't know if it is the lasting effects of the illness from our ocean voyage or the grimy film on the windows of the train, but the landscape looks dull and flat. Where are the mountains, like the ones I knew from Pereto that wrapped around our village like a green velvet collar?

The towns we pass through look gray, the buildings shoddy and badly constructed—nothing like the great cathedrals in the eternal cities of Italy and France that we passed through on our way to Le Havre. Everything appears to be made out of wood. There are monstrous buildings, factories perhaps, or warehouses. What does America have in such quantity that it needs such big buildings? Cheaply made buildings, too, with no sense of permanence. And surrounding every town, along the sullen miles of railroad track, are the backs of sad little houses, each with its own rickety outhouse planted in weeds and surrounded by piles of junk. Every structure looks like something waiting to burn down. Nothing like the solid stone dwellings of my home.

To me, these ugly American settlements seem half-hearted and temporary, like camps thrown together by conquering armies before they move to their next battle.

My brother Stefano seems wide-eyed and full of excitement, seeing the best of everything where I can only see the worst. All around me, voices are chattering in a half dozen languages, which delight and amaze my brother, but these noises fill me with emptiness and dread. I motion to a fellow passenger to open the window, making a lifting gesture with my hands, hoping to relieve the stench of human bodies in our cramped compartment. I wonder, how will anyone in this country know I am a man, a person of experience and intelligence, when I cannot make my words understood and have to point and gesture like a fool?

By prearrangement with our *padrone,* we are met at the train station in Milford. We are stinking of sweat, not the good honest sweat of hard work but the fowl stench of sea travel, exhaustion, and sickness. Our *padrone* was kind enough to bring some bread, fruit, and water, but I can barely touch it. I just want to arrive at a place with a solid floor, walls and ceiling—a place that does not move.

I am already wishing I were home in Pereto, sitting across from my wife at our simple table. I would give anything for a plain bowl of polenta, handed to me by Amalia's loving hands.

The four of us from Pereto, along with many others, are piled into open oxcarts along with our bags and delivered one by one to a series of boarding houses—plain wooden structures scattered on the eastern side of town. It seems everything is made of wood in this country, starting with the ugly rambling structure that greeted us at Ellis Island to the monotony of this town's wooden dwellings. Some are painted, some not. Everything looks gray to me. At least I am relieved to learn that our fellow travelers Giulio and Domenico will be boarding with Stefano and me, and we can finally be settled together in one place.

Our Good Name

Stefano and Giulio are eager to leave their suitcases in the room, still unpacked, and rush out to explore this new terrain. Domenico and I, the older and more weary travelers, stay behind and collapse onto our bunks.

The next day, we receive our first American breakfast. I am not accustomed to eating in the morning, and it seems very strange to eat fried eggs at the break of dawn. But I eat, just in case it is the only meal I receive for the day. I devour the toasted bread, too, and use it to sop up the runny yolk on my plate. The coffee is weak and bitter, but at least it is hot to combat the chill in the air. The weather has been chilly and damp since we arrived.

The *padrone* has come to give us a little speech and tell us our initial assignments. Our group has been assigned day jobs in construction and on farms. He explains that he will keep a portion of our paychecks every week to pay for our passage to America.

Soon, Stefano gets a full-time job at the iron foundry, the place they called the Draper Company. That's in a little town called Hopedale, right next door to Milford. Every morning, the oxcarts will come and bring a cargo of men to the Draper Company. I seem to be always among the farm workers, tilling the soil for spring planting. I am not sure this is any different from work I could do at home in Italy. Is this the great land of opportunity I heard so much about?

I had hoped to put my stonemason skills to good use at the granite quarries the town was known for. After inquiring many times, I am sent to one of the stonecutting operations in town. But I quickly see the workers they need are beasts of burden, not skilled craftsmen like me. The work is backbreaking and dangerous. I watch men much younger than me crossing over the enormous stone quarry pits by way of iron cables strung across them. They dangle by their bare hands from the cables, crossing to the other side, hand over hand. I am too old for such fearlessness.

Stefano seems to fit in easily, making friends with other young Italians who work at Draper. Men from the same villages and regions cluster together, it seems, and a surprising number in this town come from the province of Parma, as we did, or from the neighboring Piacenza province. Another large group in the town come from Le Marche, the coastal region east of Tuscany. Others are from Foggia and more southern Italian regions. I don't think anyone planned it this way, to separate into groups based on our native provinces, but it seems to happen. It is easier to speak the same familiar dialect as one's own countrymen. It is comforting to our ears.

Sometimes Stefano and his friends catch a train into Boston on a Saturday afternoon, spend the evening in the bars and burlesque shows in Scollay Square, and do whatever it is that single young men do when they are full of beer.

No one would ever spend an evening in a tavern in our home village. I think Stefano and his peers are trying to fit in, to be like other American boys.

There came a night when Stefano and two of his friends had a little too much to drink in Scollay Square and missed the last train back to Milford. All I knew was that they did not come home that night. I worried they had been assaulted, maybe killed, and left to rot in an alley somewhere in this strange and inscrutable country.

One of the friends, as Stefano would later tell me, had a cousin in the North End, and the three of them stumbled to the cousin's tenement building and pounded on the door, waking nearly everyone in the building. The cousin finally was roused from sleep and ushered the three men into his apartment, where his wife had already risen from her bed and started cooking dutifully, filling the apartment with smells of garlic and browned sausage. The three of them ate their fill and finally collapsed all together on the cousins' marital bed, where they slept and snored through the night, while their hosts were forced to squeeze into their children's beds.

It is a story Stefano would tell many times over, adding some new detail or comic twist every time. I grow tired of hearing it. Such revelries are of no interest to me. I am looking for work, home, and things of permanence. And I cannot see permanence in the work I do, whether it's loading slabs of granite or plowing the earth. Men younger than me will grow stronger at these labors. I will only grow older and weaker.

After only a few weeks of this new life, I am exhausted. I ask our *padrone* if there might be any other job for me, something more suited to a man my age, maybe indoor work like cleaning factory floors. He discourages me, saying that Italians are assigned only to certain factory jobs doing heavy lifting or dangerous work, like pouring the molten iron in the foundry. Other jobs that are easier and cleaner go to the native-born men, the Yankees who speak English.

I find it impossible to believe that a man needs to speak English in order to sweep a floor. I decide to go and see for myself. I go to the nearest factory and present myself to the front office, making clumsy pantomime gestures to indicate I will sweep the floors. I must look like the village idiot, pointing to myself, and then pretending to sweep with an invisible broom. Instead of a job, I receive a barrage of loud ugly names that I understand without any translation. The message is very clear. Italians need not apply here.

Barely a month goes by before I realize that I am nothing to these factory bosses but a strong back and a pair of hands to hold a shovel or a chisel. I am treated like a machine or an animal, a brainless thing with only one purpose. These people know nothing of me, my skills, my intelligence. They don't ask about me or inquire after my wife and my children. We are nothing more than a workers' colony, a group of low-class Italians clustered together in the eastern part of town, a section they called the Plains. It is a place where poor people live, in miserable wooden houses that creak when you climbed the stairs. I long for the solid stone houses of my native Italian village.

I try to persist as long as I can, but after just a few months, I have to tell my brother. I have made up my mind. This New Country is not for me. Its language is ugly to my ear, and I fear I will never learn it. Stefano is already mixing English words with Italian in his conversations, but I can't manage more than *hello, please,* and *thank you.*

Stefano doesn't believe me at first. It is too soon, he says. He begs me to be patient, to give it a year before deciding. But I miss my wife, my little girls, and my sweet mountain home, more precious to me than anything this land of imagined opportunity could offer. I arrange with my *padrone* to work only long enough to pay for my voyage home.

Stefano refuses to believe I am leaving. Even as he accompanies me on the train and walks with me to Boston Harbor, he holds out hope I will not leave him behind.

"There's still time to change your mind, Pietro. Please stay just a few more weeks. You might think it over a little more?"

"No, you think about it, Stefano. This place in Milford where all the Italians live, they call it the Plains, no? That means the flat place, the place with no mountains. That is no place for me. I am a child of the mountains. I am fifteen years older than you. I lived in those mountains fifteen years before you were born. My roots go deeper than yours, and they are harder to extract. I have a wife there, and four daughters, and one day, I will have sons who will work alongside me and grow strong, breathing the clean mountain air. They will have corn and potatoes on their table, yes, but much more besides. They will have pork, and chestnuts, and plums, and olive oil, and crusty bread, and wine, and all the riches the good green earth has to give.

"They will not find that here in America, my brother. And neither will I."

Part 2

The New World

Stefano, 1902

I have been in Milford for seven years. I have moved from one boarding house to another, all plain wooden houses on the eastern side of town. Some are former farmhouses, some of them built for no other purpose than to take in immigrant boarders who arrive daily by the trainload. Mostly the boarders are dusty laborers like me. We are the grunt and muscle to make the industrial gears go round.

The houses look weary, beaten down, like the men who live here. Granite workers, construction workers, farmers, factory men, day laborers. Men who wear the same dusty clothes and shoes every day. Single men, ranging in age from their teens to their forties. Some of the houses are in walking distance to the granite quarries by way of the cool, shaded paths in the old pine forest behind the houses. Down the road from these houses are the great stonecutting sheds, on the same road that heads east toward Boston. Giant slabs of Milford pink granite are loaded from there onto roaring trucks, and from there, they are transported to all the golden cities of the country. Monumental buildings like the Boston Public Library and New York Penn Station are all the product of Milford pink granite—and many calloused immigrant hands.

The boarding houses are furnished with bunk beds, as many in a room as they can fit. I share one with my cousin, Giovanni Marenghi, who is also from my native village of Pereto. He arrived in this country a few years after I did. It is good having my young cousin, twenty-four years old, to give me news of my village and to talk to me at night, just before dropping off to sleep. It is a nice distraction from the foul body odors that fill the rooms, to have someone nearby to remind me of the place I came from. It makes me feel less lonely.

One late summer evening, I am sitting on the back steps outside the house, watching Giovanni playing bocce ball with some young neighbors from the house next door. There is a handsome bocce court that some of the stone cutters have built, using the fine stone dust they had collected from the cutting sheds to line the court. The stone dust makes for a perfectly smooth, gray surface, packed down hard and solid.

There is a pretty girl, maybe fifteen or sixteen years old, and two younger boys at the bocce court. While I watch them play, a man comes and sits beside me.

"*Buona sera, paesano*! I am Luigi, and those are my children—Celestina, Giovanni, and Giuseppe. That other boy—he is your son?"

"No, no, he is my *cugino*, from the village of Pereto. It is next to Metti and Bore."

"Ah, I see. That is not too far from my village. Varsi. Do you know it?

"Sure, Varsi. I heard of it. We are *veramente paesani*, yes. My name is Stefano Marenghi."

"Marenghi? *Madonna mia*. That is the name of my wife, Marianna Marenghi. Maybe you are related?"

"Oh, who's to say. There are so many of us. That boy, Giovanni Marenghi, he comes from my village, and I call him my cousin, but I can't tell you how he's related to me! I have no idea. He was one of three Giovanni Marenghis born in our little village, all within two years of each other, from three different families. I can't keep track of them all."

Luigi laughs.

"My wife, she is from Varsi, like me. We married and had children there, in the Old Country. I traveled here alone in 1894, and every month, I sent money to my family. Then, five years later, they came here together, and now we are a family again. It makes me happy to see all my children play together like this."

We both stop to watch my cousin Giovanni patiently showing Celestina how to roll the large ball underhand, slowly and with control.

The idea is to get it as close as possible to the little ball that is rolled out first, the *pallina*. Luigi's boys are just throwing their balls out wildly, underhand and overhand, to see who can throw the hardest and farthest with no interest in the strategy of the game at all.

"They look good together, no?" Luigi asks me. "A nice young couple." He is talking about his daughter and my cousin Giovanni.

But I am looking only at Celestina. What a pretty name—the perfect name for such a celestial being. Her face is shaped like a heart, and long waves of chestnut hair frame her face. Her hips are a little plump but not too much, their width accentuated by her tiny waist. She is beautiful but not frail. Strong, but in a feminine way. In my mind, she is just the kind of woman I had always pictured as the woman I would marry someday.

She reminds me of the sweet golden plums that grew near my childhood house. They had a little crease down the side, where I would tear the fruit open and expose the luscious sweetness inside. This girl is like that, fresh and full of life. I am at an age when my mind turns more and more to marriage and family—and a woman who will bear me many fine sons.

"Stefano? What do you think, Stefano?"

"What do I think? Think of what?"

"Your cousin, and my Celestina. A pretty couple, no?"

"Oh, yes. Yes, Luigi. Your daughter, she is a very pretty girl."

I pull out my pipe and a little tin of tobacco from my shirt pocket. Smoking my pipe is the one thing I can always count on to calm me. Luigi watches me fill the bowl of the pipe and tamp it down, then carefully light the mixture with my hand cupped around the flame to shield it from the wind. The sweet flavor of the smoke feels warm and good in my mouth.

"Tell me, Stefano. When did you come over?"

"I came in 1895 with my older brother Pietro."

"And where is Pietro now?"

"Ah, he did not stay. He went home. He had a wife and four little girls waiting for him. Now he has two little boys, too."

"But why did he go back?"

"I wanted him to stay. I thought he would settle here, and then, after a time, he would send for his wife and children, just as you did. But he was older than me—forty years old when he came here. It is an age when a man comes to expect more from life. More respect, I think. More than he was able to find in this country."

I pause to take a puff or two on my pipe and continue. "Pietro was a man with great intelligence and skill, a fine stonemason. He can make a house where the stones fit together so tight, you don't need any mortar. But he couldn't find that kind of work here, doing the work he knew best. In our village, he is a man of honor, very respected.

"He tried to get a job sweeping floors—can you imagine? A man like that, with talent and experience, asking to sweep floors. But when he opened his mouth, only Italian words came out. A man shouted at him, 'No guinea wops here!' He understood those bad words. Some of the few English words he ever learned.

"So he went back to his wife, Amalia. And he had more to go back to than I would ever have. As the older son, you know, he inherits everything—the house where we grew up and the land. But I had nothing to go back to. My future—my only future—is here."

"You miss your brother, Stefano?"

I look away. I can't answer. I remember embracing Pietro for the last time at the dock at Boston Harbor and watching him get lost in the crowd of Italian men boarding the ship to go home. He was one of the many *ritornati*. Those who returned.

I don't want to think about Pietro. It will make tears come to my eyes. I had a foolish tendency to cry easily. So I change the subject.

"And what about you, Luigi? You have brothers and sisters?"

"I was the first child, but my mother died giving birth to me. The day I was baptized at the church, there was a funeral mass for my mother, the same church, the same day. She was just twenty-two years old. My father quickly married again and had more children, so I have a half-brother and a half-sister. I think my father always blamed me for the loss of his first wife. He told me I looked like her. That was not a good thing. He never showed me the same tenderness he showed to his other children.

"When I was eleven years old, my stepmother died in childbirth, too, and this time, the baby died with her. This made my father a very dark man. I tried to be a good son, to work the land with him and help put food on the table, but I could never please my father. I did not find any happiness until I married Marianna. We made a home with Marianna's mother, and I was blessed with three children of my own. I never went back to my father's house again."

"Your father is still living, Luigi?"

"I don't know. It doesn't matter to me. I will never go back."

"I'm sorry, Luigi."

"No, no need to be sorry. I have much to look forward to here. You know, my wife, Marianna, she is expecting another child."

"Luigi! That is good news! Congratulations to you!"

"*Si, grazie.* We are very happy. We will have our first American child. And soon, we will need a new place to live, too. With three children, and soon one more, the apartment here is very small. Maybe we will see if there is a bigger apartment in that place on Reade Street, the one they call the stone castle."

"Yes, I hear that is a good place. They welcome Italians, and the owner is Italian. Or maybe you will have a house. I will make you a bet, Luigi. I will have a house one day soon, and you will have a house near mine. We will be neighbors, and both our houses will be full of children and grandchildren. You remember my words. You will see."

"You make me smile, Stefano. You dream the big dreams of a young man."

"They are same as your dreams, my friend, are they not? The same as every man who ever crossed an ocean to make a home in a new country. It is a dream for a future. For a better life for our families. Don't you think all our dreams are the same?"

I puff on my pipe and turn again to watch Celestina as she grasps the heavy ball in both hands and gracefully launches it forward. The arch and curve of her back. The long sure extension of her graceful arms. The effortless wave of her hand to brush the hair from her face as she watches the rolling ball.

Perfection.

As the evening sky dims, Luigi stands up and announces it is time for his children to go to bed. I watch him gather his two sons and his daughter and shepherd them into the neighboring house. He calls out *Buona notte* to me and waves before disappearing inside.

Giovanni puts the bocce balls away on the wooden rack and comes to sit down next to me on the steps.

"So, Giovanni," I ask, "what do you think of the girl?"

"Who? You mean Celestina? She is a child."

"A child who is old enough to marry!"

"I was just playing with children, a little girl and her brothers. I have no interest in her."

I will say no more. I do not want to put thoughts into his head that are not already there, only to make a rival of a much younger cousin. Let him think he has all the time in the world to find a wife. Let him take his time. For me, time is a little more precious. I have to move more quickly.

––––––––––––––

Every evening, I watch from my window to see if Celestina is in the yard behind our houses, hoping I might see her taking in the laundry from the clothesline or pulling up dandelion greens for a supper salad. If I catch a glimpse of her, I quietly go out to the back steps, pretending to be engrossed in smoking my pipe, acting as if I don't notice her, my eyes cast down. Does she know I am playing this game with her?

It is only when her father appears that I feel the courage to approach their house. It is not proper to speak to a young woman without her father or mother present. Luigi always thinks I am coming to talk with him, but my whole body is leaning toward Celestina. I always inquire politely about his wife Marianna, a woman I have never seen. Luigi always replies that she is tired and resting in bed, that her pregnancy is weighing heavily on her. She is forty years old, a difficult age to be with child.

When I arrive home from work one Friday in September, I learn that little Maria Abretti has finally arrived in this world. The following afternoon, I quietly approach their door, holding a small basket of pears I had planned to leave at their doorstep, but Luigi hears me shuffling outside the door and welcomes me inside.

"Ah, it is you, my friend! *Benvenuto!*"

"Congratulations, Luigi. How is the new mother?"

"She is resting. No one in the house has slept. Little Maria is quiet all day and waits until dark to let us know the strength of her lungs. She will be an opera singer, that one!"

He beckons me to follow him through a small parlor to the bedroom. Marianna is sitting up in bed, propped up against her pillows, wearing a nightdress and a woolen shawl. Her hair is loose and limp around her face. And there, sitting beside the bed in a small chair, Celestina is cradling the newborn child in her arms.

I cannot tell you the passion it stirs in me, to see this beautiful girl as I have imagined her a hundred times. She is exactly as I picture my future wife, holding my future child.

"Marianna, this is my friend, Stefano Marenghi, the one I told you about. Look what he brought for you. Such beautiful pears!"

"*Buona sera, Signora,*" I say, bowing my head slightly toward her. But she seems too weak to move. With some effort, she utters, "*Grazie,*" in a barely audible whisper.

Luigi pulls up a chair for me, but the only person in the room I can see is Celestina. I could never have imagined that the sight of a young woman cradling a child could be so arousing. I try to turn my attention to the new mother, Marianna, out of courtesy, but she appears very old, as if the newborn child has aged her beyond her years. Her hair is dull and needs brushing. I try to make polite conversation, but I feel I am only adding to the poor mother's weariness. And the distraction of their older daughter is almost unbearable. I cannot sit still any longer. I finally stand up, congratulate Luigi and Marianna, and quietly leave.

In the weeks that follow, I again ask my cousin Giovanni if the girl next door interests him. He shrugs and insists Celestina is only a child, far too young for him. For that matter, it doesn't appear as if any young woman interests him. I begin to wonder if Giovanni will be that one person in our family who will never marry, the one so many families seem to have, who goes off to become a priest or lives the life of solitary bachelorhood.

One doesn't ask another man about such things.

Having satisfied myself that my cousin is not my rival, I then begin to worry about all the other single men that occupy our boarding house. In my mind, Celestina is like an innocent lamb, like the little lamb Angelina I had loved so much in my childhood, and these men with their sweaty clothes and coarse manners are a pack of hungry wolves. Celestina is not safe from them. I must take it upon myself to be her protector.

On a cool October evening, I knock on Luigi's door and ask to speak with him privately. He follows me down the stairs and I stop in the small foyer. My mouth is dry, and I am having difficulty speaking.

"Stefano, is something wrong, my friend?"

I cannot answer. I am losing my courage. But I reach into my jacket pocket, and the object waiting there gives me strength.

I pull out a small, brown velvet box, very old and frayed from age. I open it to reveal a cameo brooch made of finely-carved carnelian shell and studded with tiny pearls around its gold oval frame.

"It is a cameo, Luigi. It belonged to my mother. God rest her soul. I wish to give it to Celestina, as a symbol of my honorable intentions. With all respect, I ask your permission for this."

Luigi seems confused. "You mean—you wish to marry my daughter?"

I study his face, trying to understand his reaction. "Yes, Luigi. I do."

"Forgive me, I need to ask. How old are you, my friend?"

"I am thirty-two."

"You are twice her age, Stefano. You are closer to my age than you are to my daughter's."

"Luigi, I assure you. I am still young and strong, and I work hard. Someday, very soon, I will give Celestina the finest house in town, and I will build it with my own hands. I will love her and protect her as no other man could ever do."

Luigi pauses for a moment and studies me.

"You surprise me, my friend. But I believe you are an honorable man. A serious man. I will give this box to Celestina and ask her what is in her heart. If she will have you, then you have my blessing. If she refuses you, I will return the box to you."

"I ask nothing more."

A week passes, and then another. I wait anxiously until finally I can wait no more. I see Luigi return from work one evening, and I stop him outside the boarding house.

"Luigi, I must know. What does Celestina say to my offer?"

"You must be patient, my friend. She is young, and this is a heavy decision. And she is consumed by her chores, caring for my wife and our newborn child. She can think of nothing else but to be a help to her mother. So you see, she is a good girl."

"But when, Luigi? When will I know?"

"Patience, my friend. Please be patient."

And so, I wait. I am patient. Days go by without a word. But the next time I see Luigi, he has a long face. Without saying a word, he hands me back the brown velvet box. "What? She refuses me? She will not have me?"

"She is not ready, Stefano."

It is unthinkable. I cannot bear to look at the box. In my mind, I have already decided that this is the brooch Celestina will wear on her wedding day. On the day she will marry me, and no one but me.

"No, I will not take it back. Tell Celestina to hold it for me and keep it safe."

"But it is much too precious. She cannot accept it."

"Please tell her to hold onto it."

"My friend, let me give some advice to you. You are a much older man. You could take advantage of a young girl, put pressure on her when she is too young to know her mind. I will not let that happen. When she is ready, she will let us know. Until then, you will respect my daughter."

"I will, Luigi. *Ho capito.*"

As he walks away, I cannot help but think that I would protect my own daughters some day in exactly the same manner. A man understands the hunger that burns in the hearts of other men and naturally stands between that and his daughters. But yet, I sense a bit of hope. Not a definite "no," but a request for more time. Perhaps, in time, Celestina will be ready to marry, and she might yet accept me. In time.

As heavy flakes of January snow descend one Sunday afternoon, I hatch an idea. I have seen the children make snowmen in the town, something I had never seen in my home village. I decide I will make a very special snow woman in honor of Celestina. A statue to her beauty, like a white marble statue of a goddess. I will erect this snow statue right in front of her apartment house.

The work is harder than I imagined. I don't want the snow woman to be too fat and insult my Celestina, but if it is too thin it will not stand. I make three snow boulders in different sizes, the way I have seen children do, rolling each ball in the snow until it gets bigger and bigger. I fill out the bottom one to resemble a full skirt. Instead of sticks for arms, I try to mold two arms close to her body, as if her hands are folded in front of her. And on her head, I add bunches of pine branches, the pine needles resembling her hair. It looks a little foolish, perhaps, but I trust Celestina will be impressed with my diligent labor and my good intentions.

I have just wrapped my scarf around her neck and am about to begin sculpting the blank face when Celestina appears at the front steps with a blue knit shawl draped loosely over her shoulders.

"What do you think you are doing? My neighbors told me you were out here making a fool of yourself. What is wrong with you? Are you drunk? Are you crazy? *Sei pazzo?*

I stand transfixed by her, and by her fury. Her frozen breath forms a halo around her head. She is from another world.

"Do you think this will impress me? Do you think I am a simple-minded child? I will show you what I think of your foolishness."

In one dramatic gesture, she swipes off the snow woman's head with a powerful back-hand blow and shoves the snow woman's torso to the ground. She kicks and kicks the bottom boulder, but it doesn't seem to budge. Finally, she reaches inside her blouse and pulls out the brown velvet box.

"And you can have this! Do you think you can impress me with trinkets? Do you think I can be bought? I am not for sale!"

She throws the box at my head. It hits its target. But I do not flinch.

Over and over, she picks up chunks of snow and hurls them at me. I am covered with snow. I imagine I look more like a snowman than the one I just created.

Frozen and awestruck, I watch her face redden and her hair fly. I could weep at such furious beauty. The fire in her eyes fills me with unbearable joy and kicks me in the stomach at the same time. Now *that* is a woman!

She pauses her attack and stops to look at me. She seems confused by my complete lack of movement and my unwavering stare.

"What is wrong with you, you stupid man? Are you drunk? *Ubriaco*?"

"Celestina! You are magnificent!" I wrap my snow-caked arms around her and hold her tightly. I swear to her I will never let her go.

The next time I see my mother's cameo brooch, it is fastened to the throat of Celestina's high-collared wedding dress. On April 12, 1903, Celestina and I stand side by side before Father Hanrahan at the altar of St. Mary's. She looks like an angel, my celestial one. My Celestina.

Our son Bartolomeo is born six months later.

Celestina, 1903

It's a curse to be the oldest daughter. A curse.

As long as I can remember, I take care of my little brothers. The two little princes, I call them. I was no more than a girl myself when I was changing little Giovanni's diapers in Varsi. Now here we are in the New Country, and what does my mother do? She has to go ahead and have yet another baby. At the age of forty! What was she thinking? I'm a newly married woman, expecting a child of my own, and I'm still changing and washing diapers for my mother's baby.

Stefano found a vacant apartment in the same building as my parents, as if that were some kind of advantage. What advantage? It's good for my mother but not for me. She had a hard pregnancy at her age. So she's still spending most of her days in bed while I look after my nine-month-old sister Maria, washing her diapers by hand in the sink, bathing and feeding her every day. I should be thinking about my own baby, not my mother's.

I am too young to be a *casalinga*—a poor housewife. An unpaid domestic servant, no better off than a mule. That's all I am.

Every night, I cook for seven people. My mother complains she feels poorly all the time, so the job of cooking falls to me. I make a big pot of minestrone with whatever vegetables are to be had, and I serve it to my husband, my parents, and my two younger brothers. All the while, I am tending to baby sister Maria, who fidgets on my lap. I barely have a moment to eat a single bite.

You think this is easy? What about me? When do I get to rest? This baby growing inside me wants me to feed him, too. I can feel him sucking my energy from me, as if my umbilical cord were a siphon.

I have a fatigue in my bones that no one my age should ever have to feel. I should be the one lying down, with my mother looking after *me*.

If I tell my mother I'm tired, she tells me it's my own fault. Fooling around with an older man and getting in trouble at the age of sixteen. But what would she know? Shriveled old woman. What would she know about being a young girl and receiving the soft kiss of an older man, on a cold winter's night, alone in the dark stairwell? What would she know about that surprising new feeling, as if Stefano's kiss had ignited a fuse that burned directly from my lips, pouring its heat down my throat to my breasts to the center of my body, melting me between my legs? What would she know about pushing him to the wall, tearing open my coat and blouse, and lifting my skirt to this strange little red-haired man?

When I missed my next monthly blood, I told Stefano. We had no choice but to get married. Two months later, I was his wife. And I know I brought it on myself. But I don't like to talk to my mother about such things. She wouldn't understand a young woman's desires.

She couldn't manage without me. But is she grateful? No, never. Always criticizing me, her only daughter and helper.

My baby boy arrives in October 1903, only a year after my sister Maria was born. I knew long before he was born that he would be named Bartolomeo, in honor of my husband's father. That's the Italian way. And the first girl would be named after Stefano's mother, Elisabetta. So I already knew the names of my first son and first daughter before they were born.

My Bartolomeo arrives into this world screaming, even while his aunt Maria, a baby herself, is wailing loudly in the other room, wondering why no one is giving her any attention. When will I ever get the sound of screeching babies out of my ears? At least the midwife could hold Bartò for a little while and let me close my eyes for a few minutes. Stefano is crying tears of joy, holding his hands over his heart, saying, "I have a son! I have a son!"

As if *he* deserves all the credit. I'm the one who did all the work!

Our Good Name

The first few months, you cannot imagine the chaos in my little apartment, which is barely big enough for Stefano and me. I can rely on my mother to come by while Stefano and Luigi are at work, but not to help me. She expects me to fix her tea and serve her sweet biscotti, with me holding my nursing baby at my breast. Little Maria always comes with her, and soon, she is walking—a dangerous new development. Her chubby little legs propel her all around our little apartment, walking, crawling, rolling, and other forms of locomotion I cannot describe, all with a surprising speed.

Sometimes Maria likes to pull the curtains down, still attached to their rod, bringing everything crashing to the floor. Other times she will crawl under the kitchen table and find a way to knock over a chair. Her favorite spot is the bed I share with my husband, which my mother never fails to notice is not neatly made. Maria is always trying to climb onto my bed, only to get tangled up in the sheets and ends up falling with a loud thud onto the floor.

After a few months of living like this, Stefano can see the rage building up inside me, not because he is very observant but because I make sure to let him know.

"You need to do something, Stefano, before I throw both babies out the window! And my mother, too!"

Stefano listens carefully to me when I tell him that the last thing he wants is an unhappy wife in his house. He is beginning to understand the woman he has married. So he comes up with an idea. He writes a letter to his brother Pietro back in his home village and asks him to send one of his five daughters to America to stay with us and help me with the baby. After all, Pietro has so many daughters. It seems obvious that he could spare at least one of them to help me.

One of Pietro's daughters is more than happy to make the journey to America. Albina, fifteen years old, will make the crossing in May 1904 with her friend, Maria Volpicelli, who is from the same village and close to Albina in age. Maria has family already living in Milford, on River Street, and she plans to stay with them. Maria also has something else—a handsome older brother named Domenico, a young stonemason from Metti who now lives in Milford. I have seen him. He is dark and square-faced and has a thick moustache. I am sure the prospect of seeing Domenico in America is a much greater enticement to Albina than being a household helper to me.

When Albina arrives in town, we send word for her to come see her Uncle Stefano and to meet me, her Aunt Celestina, as soon as she is settled. Stefano has not seen her since she was six years old, and he greets her with a warm embrace, as if she were his own daughter. Stefano tells my parents we have an important guest, and they all squeeze into our little apartment, my parents, my brothers, and my baby sister.

Albina has brought Italian sweets for everyone, bars of soft white torrone and hazelnut-filled chocolates, which make her popular with my younger brothers, Giovanni and Giuseppe. It is soon clear that she has experience caring for little ones. When she scoops up my baby sister Maria in her arms and holds her high in the air, making the child giggle, I see the look come over my mother's face. I recognize that look. The gears are spinning in her head. She is already thinking and plotting about all the things Albina can do for her.

Albina arrives at my apartment the following morning to spend the day helping me with baby Bartolomeo. I don't know how my mother senses Albina's presence, but she is soon standing at my door with Maria in her hands. My mother hands little Maria to Albina, and then drops a heavy cloth sack of foul-smelling laundry onto the floor.

"I will be busy with my sons today, and I know Maria will be much happier here with you girls. I'm sure it will make no difference to you to have one more baby in the house. And these, Celestina, are Maria's dirty diapers. You can wash them along with Bartolomeo's."

"What? You have four children, and you forget how to wash diapers yourself?"

"*Uffa!* You don't talk to your mother that way! I could have left you behind in that miserable country, but your father and I worked hard to bring you here. And this is how you talk to me, you ungrateful child?"

She does not wait for an answer and spins around to make her exit. Albina looks at me, shrugs, and bounces little Maria in her arms.

And so we begin the first of many such days, two young women, practically children ourselves, each with a baby in our arms. We cook together, and we teach each other our mothers' recipes. The recipes are similar, but each little town and each family has a particular way of doing them. Albina is three years younger than me but already a fine cook. She makes the most delicate avellini, a kind of ravioli made with pasta that is rolled so fine and thin, it is almost transparent.

I watch her while sitting at the kitchen table with Bartolomeo suckling at my breast. Albina forms a mountain of semolina flour on the table and carves out an indentation on top, so it looks like a white volcano. She drops the eggs into the indentation, then skillfully works the flour and eggs in her hands until it is a uniform mass. She makes several small balls, each the size of an orange, and rolls and rolls each ball with the rolling pin, flattening it out, folding it over onto itself, and flattening it again until the dough is impossibly thin. Just when I think it is thin enough, she holds a sheet up to the light and says, "I need to able to see my hand through it." And she keeps on rolling it thinner.

"These will be delicious stuffed with breadcrumbs and cheese and served in a plain chicken broth. I add a little nutmeg and some Parmesan."

"I make my ravioli with ricotta and Swiss chard inside. Mine are not as delicate as yours. Stefano likes to eat a whole plate of them with just butter and pepper on them."

"These avellini came out good. Maybe I will leave some with you and take some to Domenico's house for Sunday dinner?"

"Ah, Domenico. I was wondering when you would mention him. Does he like your cooking?"

"I hope so! All these hours of work to make a soup that he will consume in three gulps. But his mother is kind. She makes him compliment my cooking in case he forgets."

"He is why you came to America, isn't he? Not to clean diapers with me?" Albina simply looks up at me and tries to suppress a grin.

"Has he ever kissed you, Albina? You want to marry him?" I give her a sideways look, tilt my head, and bat my eyelashes to tease her.

"Stop asking me questions! I am too young for this kind of talk. I am only fifteen."

"Albina, I am an experienced married lady, and I will give you some advice. If you want him, you need to let him know. Domenico grew up with you. He knows you since you are a baby. He probably thinks you're still a little girl. Don't wait for him to make a move. You kiss him first."

"I can't do that! It's not right!"

"I tell you, Albina, men are all thick in the head. They don't understand anything you say if you don't speak to them VERY LOUDLY. And if that doesn't work, you have to hit them on the side of the head to make your point."

Now Albina is giggling loudly.

"I also know a third approach that is the most effective of all. This is for later, when you are married. It has to do with not allowing him into your bed. That works really well."

"*Zia Celestina!* You are very bad! Very bad!"

I don't know what I would do without Albina to get me through these days of caring for two babies, my sister and my son. I would have liked a sister like Albina, close to my age, someone I can talk to. I can empty my soul to her. I hate to see her leave each evening after Stefano comes home.

We pay Albina by feeding her and giving her food to take home to the Volpicelli family. Sometimes we give her a little money when we have it. I know it won't be enough to keep her here with me forever.

When my little Bartò is a year old and starts walking, Albina starts taking piecework at the straw hat factory, so I see her less and less. I miss her company during the long days, with no one but babies to talk to. Albina is my niece, but I made her stop calling me *Zia* long ago. She will always have a place in my heart and home as my close friend.

Before 1904 ends, I find out I am going to have another baby. It is hard for me to imagine a second baby in our tiny apartment, especially with my sister Maria under foot all the time. Maria is now an energetic two-year-old, capable of more destruction in the space of a minute than any child I have ever known. And always, Maria would look up at me after breaking a bowl or spoiling the freshly washed sheets and smile so sweetly, I cannot bear to scold her. It isn't her fault that our mother deposits her here, a mother who loves her boys more than she ever loved her girls.

It is time once again to plant an idea into Stefano's head. I remind him of a promise he made to my father when he was courting me. He promised he would build me a house, the biggest house in the Plains. I know he can do it. He has saved some money. He thinks I don't know, but I found the tobacco tin he had stuffed into the mattress at the foot of the bed. What an obvious place to hide money, in the mattress. That man has no imagination! And I know he has worked hard for years, spending almost nothing on himself, putting aside every dollar he could for his future wife and family.

Well, now that family is looking him in the face. *Remember, Stefano, when you courted me, what you promised? Remember Stefano?*

Stefano, 1905

"Mr. Tracey, why are you smiling at me like that?"

"Mr. Marenghi, maybe you think we are not much alike. But I understand who you are. You are an immigrant, as my mother and father once were half a century ago, when they came from Ireland to escape the Hunger. I know what it meant to my mother and father to buy this land, to own property in this new country. And I know what it now means to you."

I am not accustomed to seeing an Irishman smiling at me. It is already strange enough to be sitting in a lawyer's office and signing a legal paper for the first time. But stranger still to be looked on with kindness by Irish eyes. The Irish were once like us, hungry immigrants, or so I am told. They were unwanted and insulted in this strange New World. Now most of them look at us Italians with scorn, as if we are to blame for taking the jobs they fought so hard for.

One by one, Irish families like the Traceys have been moving out of the Plains section of town, moving to houses further uptown, and Italian families are moving in. The Irish families seem to be running away from us. We have no great love for each other. It will be many years before the Italians and Irish start to realize we are all Catholics. We have more in common with each other than we do with the Yankees who were here before us.

Yes, the Irish were immigrants once, too, but they spoke the language of the townspeople when they came here. Already they are sitting in places of power, in the town hall, in banks and businesses uptown. They are schoolteachers and principals. They are bosses in the factories.

I wonder how many generations it will take for my own family to have education and business connections and move to nice big houses uptown.

———————

My lawyer tells me where to sign my name, with Celestina as my witness. It is a note for $1,100. The loan is payable with interest to Mr. Tracey in one year's time. That's when 7 Hayward Street will be completely ours.

I have been eyeing this land for years. When I first arrived in America, I lived in many boarding houses, including one at 47 Hayward Street, and I passed by this pretty piece of land every day on my way to work. There are already some buildings on the property, a sad little cottage and a small barn, plus an outhouse in the back. The Traceys rented out the cottage to a French-Canadian family in recent years.

The cottage is one open room furnished with little more than a pot-belly stove and a soapstone sink. It will be enough to shelter us until I can build us a good strong permanent house. It is a triple lot with enough land for three houses, but I picture only one: a grand three-story house surrounded by fruit trees, grape arbors, and gardens. It will have a wide front porch where we will sit together and greet our neighbors as they walk by. And I will build a handsome stone wall along the front border, the way my brother taught me, to tell the world that the whole length of this land belongs to one family alone.

My father-in-law, Luigi Abretti, and his wife Marianna sign a deed just two weeks later for a property across the street from us. They have their boys Giovanni and Giuseppe still living with them and their girl Maria.

It is just as I had once predicted. Luigi and I are neighbors.

I am in my thirty-fifth year, with a young wife and a baby boy, and one more child on the way. Celestina is a good solid girl, and young enough to bear many more children. My greatest wish is for a house with children in every room and many hands helping each other. We will need a big house for our growing family and for all the relatives who will come to visit us from the Old Country to admire our good fortune.

Maybe I am doing this for Pietro most of all. I want to show my brother that I have made a good life here in the New Country. Maybe he will be persuaded to come back and visit if I have a big, beautiful home. Maybe, if I am honest, I hope to impress him, to show off a little bit. Every time I write him a letter, I ask him when he is going to come visit me and meet my young family. It has been ten years since I saw him, and I have never lost hope that he will surprise me one day by appearing at my door. In the meantime, he sends his daughters to America, one by one, until the boys in his house back in Pereto outnumber the girls.

Luigi Abretti and I have a bet. Both of us already have modest structures on our property, but both of us will be building new houses on our land. Which one of us will finish first? It will take years. We are both working full-time as laborers; I am still at the iron foundry, and Luigi is doing farm work. We both have to build our houses in our spare time, little by little, getting help from others where we can but doing most of the heavy labor ourselves. I am determined that my house will be much bigger than Luigi's, maybe the biggest house on the street, but even so, I wager that my house will be finished first.

We start building in the summer of 1905. My first task is to dig a deep cellar, with thick walls of stone and an earthen floor to keep it cool and dry all year. There will be a root cellar for beets, carrots, potatoes, and butternut squash, and plenty of shelves for canned tomatoes, pickled vegetables, preserved fruits, sacks of dried beans, cornmeal, and flour. The back end of the cellar will have deep wooden bins for wine bottles. We will make our own wine, the way my father did, crushed from our own grapes.

The hunger that drove me from my native village will never visit me again. I will never go hungry in my new house. Nor will any of my children. Never.

The front entry will have big double doors with brass doorknobs and long oval windows in etched glass with lace curtains. Those doors will open to a wide hall and a grand staircase. There will be a row of little parlors along the hall for visitors, a big kitchen in the back, and a dining room with a heavy mahogany table and caned chairs. The second floor will have bedrooms for everyone, including the biggest bedroom in the back for Celestina and me and a stairway up to a full attic where we can dry and cure our own hams and sausages in the winter months, when the attic is cool and dry.

It is a labor of love. As my father once told me, the work is always sweeter when you are working for yourself. I whistle and sing Italian arias as I dig the cellar, working every evening, every Sunday. I cover it nightly with tarps weighted down with lengths of lumber to keep the rainwater out.

Before long, I realize my family will have to move out of the little cottage in the back. We will have to start living in the newly dug cellar so we can use the little house to store lumber, plaster, building supplies, and anything we need to keep dry. By now, the back part of the cellar is covered with wide wooden planks laid over the crossbeams that will support the floor above it. It forms a kind of crude shelter, although dark as a cave, where my young family has begun sleeping on warm summer nights.

All I can see in my mind's eye is the finished house, and every step along the way looks beautiful to me. But others passing by can't see it yet. They don't see what I can see.

Every Sunday afternoon, a parade of buggies rolls down East Main Street occupied by rich ladies from uptown showing off their best Sunday dresses, lace parasols, and broad flowered hats. Their drivers turn onto Hayward Street and stop the buggies along the road so the ladies can sit and stare at us as if we are animals in a zoo. It is an entertainment for them, to see how the foreigners live. Or maybe they are impressed with my singing?

I can't hear everything they say, but I can tell what is in their hearts from the smirks on their faces, the fingers pointing, their haughty glances.

"Oh, look, Sarah, they're actually living down there in that hole, like burrowing animals. They're even breeding little mongrels, too."

"What a disgrace. My horses have a prettier sleeping chamber than they do."

"They're all criminals, you know. The dregs of Europe. Those Italians ship their very worst from their filthy slums and dump them like garbage on our shores. It's a shame they're allowed to breed like that, like disgusting rats."

"There ought to be a law."

I try to pretend they aren't there. I have too much work to do, and their taunts only strengthen my resolve to build a house those ladies will envy one day. A house that will make their uptown houses look shabby. But Celestina has a shorter fuse. One day, after clearing weeds with a sickle all morning, she sees one of the carriages pulling up and marches toward it with that sharp weapon in her hand, screaming profanities that would be clear and understandable in any language. The ladies in the carriage shriek, and with a crack of a whip, the horse speeds away.

It takes years, but my house is rising higher and higher into the clouds. There comes a time when I feel satisfied that my house is finished. I think it is beautiful, chocolate brown, with clean white shutters and window frames and white columns on the front porch like something from a Roman temple. There is still some wallpaper to hang, maybe a few finishing touches, but just as I had promised my wife, we have the biggest, finest house on Hayward Street.

My family is still sleeping every night on the first floor while waiting for the fresh paint to dry on the second floor. But I think I am ready to show off my upstairs bedrooms to Luigi and Marianna. I ask them to come over and see for themselves that my work is finally done. I know they will admire the beautiful, paneled doors, the stairs with the dark mahogany banister, and the varnished oak floors.

"Luigi, you haven't seen the second floor yet. Come, come. Marianna, be careful of the stairs, and don't get any wet paint on your skirt."

I stand at the end of the hall watching them inspect the bedrooms one by one, expecting them to emerge with abundant praise. But Luigi is shaking his head as he circles back to me.

"Stefano, I don't think you are finished yet. You forgot to make the closets."

"Closets? What closets? Who needs closets? You hang your pants on a hook at night. You put your shoes under the bed. In the morning you put your shoes and pants back on."

"American houses have closets!"

"*Madonna mia!*" I mutter, descending the stairs. "Celestina, come here. Did you forget to tell me to make the closets?"

"What closets?" she roars back. "Italian houses don't have closets. Maybe a chest of drawers, a wardrobe. I'll put a clothesline in the attic, and we can hand our extra clothes up there. Who needs closets?"

That settles that. My Celestina. She always gets the last word.

Celestina, 1908

My brother-in-law Pietro was more than eager to send his daughters to America. He kept the boys Uggero and Mario to himself, those precious sons he so longed for and waited more than a dozen years to have. But he was happy to release his daughters to the New World like so many birds flung to the eastern winds.

Maria Rosa is Pietro's second daughter to make the crossing. We call her Rosina. She missed her sister Albina's wedding to Domenico in January because she was afraid to make the voyage in the dead of winter. But she is now just a short walk from her big sister on Parkhurst Street. She can see her any time she wants.

I worry all the time about Rosina. She is only six years younger than me, but she makes me feel like her wise old grandmother. She needs me to look out for her. She is such a pretty thing—tiny, shy, like a little girl. Her hair is a dark chestnut brown that shows sparks of red in the sun. I know she will attract the hungry eyes of men.

After just a year in this country, she is now more woman than girl, fuller at the chest and hips and narrower at the waist. Just like my shape used to be, before three babies made me thick as a loaf of bread in the middle.

In addition to helping me with my three little ones—Bartolomeo, Elisabetta, and my five-month-old Girolamo—Rosina starts working at the straw factory where they make ladies' hats. We call it the "shop." That's when I really started to worry for her. So many men work there, and I worry Rosina won't know how to handle them. She is too soft, too easy, just like my poor husband.

Sure enough, she comes home one day looking like she woke up and discovered something about the world she didn't want to know.

"So, what happened down the shop today?"

Silence. Sometimes girls forget how to speak when they get upset. I was never like that, but some of my friends sometimes need a little push to make them talk.

"Something happen to you, Rosina? Tell me."

Reluctantly, she starts to talk.

"Today, *Zia*, I was just coming back from the toilet. They only give a few minutes for us to pee every day, and I was last in line, so I had to run to get back to my worktable. I did not pay attention, I was in such a hurry. I didn't see the big arm reaching out, grabbing me. It pulled me into the room where men pee.

"What a smell—so much worse than the women's toilets. No one was in there but this man and me. I saw it was the foreman. My boss! What can I do? He pushed me against the wall and squeezed my breasts so hard, like I am some kind of plaything. He tried to reach inside my shirt, tears the top buttons off, and I started to scream. He said, 'You want your job? You want to keep your job? You shut your mouth if you know what's good for you.'"

"*Bastardo*! I will kill him myself, with my bare hands!"

"No, *Zia*, no, let me finish. There is a man, he saw what happened. His name is Giuseppe. Big strong man. Giuseppe Tolenti, I think. He saw what happened. He came in and grabbed the boss and pushed him outside. Without looking at me, out of respect, he said he will wait outside and guard the door until I fixed myself up. I tied my shawl in front, so it covered my torn blouse."

At this, she unties the shawl to reveal the missing buttons on her shirt.

"That beast! I will kill him!"

"No, *Zia*, no. There's nothing you can do. Giuseppe say this man bothers the girls all the time. They tell the girls, if you don't like it, you can get a job someplace else. Giuseppe going to be in trouble, too, because he disrespect the boss."

"Who is this, Giuseppe?"

"I don't know. Big man, thick neck. Old. Very old. Thirty years old, I think."

"*O dio mio.* He too old for you. Is he *bass' italiano?*"

"I don't know, *Zia.* Why is that important? He protect me."

"Never mind! You stay away from old men and *bass' italiani!* I'll tell you what to do. Next time you go to work, you tie your hair back, put it under a scarf. No one needs to see your pretty hair. And besides, long pretty hair sometimes gets caught in the machines. Did you see what happened to your friend Giuseppina? She get her hair caught in a machine down the shop, and now her face is all pulled to one side, permanently. Now she looks like a monster the rest of her life.

"You keep your hair pulled back. Maybe your boss won't recognize you. And I will give you a big strong hat pin. That will be your weapon. You use it next time. Just in case you don't have a big thick-necked man to protect you. Stab the bastard good, right in the part where it hurts!"

I point to the place between my legs, making a stabbing motion, and this makes my niece blush a little and laugh in a nervous way.

"Okay," I say, "now you feel better. And since you've been crying already, you chop up the onions for supper. I go get some more from the cellar."

I slip away to get some more onions and a couple of jars of my canned tomatoes from the cellar shelves. Before I go back up, I sit on the wooden steps and rest a few minutes.

I think about Rosina all the time. Lost little lamb. What would she do without me to teach her all about men and the way it is in the world? My mamma never spent two minutes talking to me about anything. Always fussing over her boys, never for me. Sometimes I wish I could take all the men, my brothers included, and put them on a big boat back to the Old Country. All the problems of the world are caused by men.

I'll keep an eye on Rosina. I'll protect her.

Our Good Name

The next morning, I get up early to watch Rosina pin up her hair on top of her head and completely cover it with a kerchief, tied tightly at the nape of her neck. I help her tuck a few loose curls under the kerchief. Now not a single hair is showing. I hand her an old gray shawl of mine, threadbare and drab. Maybe this way, her boss won't even recognize her.

"And you didn't forget your hatpin?"

"I don't forget. I have it here."

I watch her wrap the shawl around her shoulders and help her fasten the front with the pin. It has a thick bronze shaft about six inches long with a little cap to cover the pointed end. The head of the pin is decorated with a bronze-plated miniature carnation.

"Let me fix the pin so the pointy end is inside the shawl. That way, no one sees how long it is. There. Now you only see the carnation on top. It looks like just a pretty pin. Perfect."

"It's okay, *Zia*. I wear a big apron over my shawl. No one will see it."

"And don't you forget to use it!"

"I won't."

"And don't you say anything to your Uncle Stefano! He worries too much."

I stand in the door as I send her off to work and watch her turn to look back at me as she steps onto the street. I call out to her, "*Coraggio, Rosina! Coraggio!*"

My good little niece. She is a smart girl. She will learn what a woman needs to do to survive among men in this world.

Late in the morning, I am standing at the kitchen sink, holding my little Girolamo in one arm as he sucks on my breast. With the other hand, I fill a heavy kettle of water from the sink and heave it to the stovetop. I start laying plates on the table. Little Elisabetta, only three years old, helps arrange the forks and spoons. Soon, Stefano will be coming in from his work in the gardens, and he will be looking for his lunch.

What would he do without me? I think to myself how stupid and helpless men are. They would all die of starvation without women to feed them.

I hear the doorknob rattling, and at first, I think it is Stefano. But no—it's Rosina. It's too early for her to be home. She bursts in the door, completely out of breath, panting. Her kerchief is missing, and her hair is loose and wild.

"Rosina! What happened? What are you doing home so soon?"

"I run, all the way. Please, *Zia*, don't make me go back."

I think she is about to collapse. Still holding my baby in my left arm, I brace Rosina's elbow with my strong right hand and guide her to the settee in the hall.

"Sit, calm yourself. I am making hot water for tea. Tell me what happened."

I squeeze in by Rosina's side and wrap my free arm around her shoulders. I don't let go and hold her tight. I make soothing sounds, like the kind you make to calm a baby, until she is able to speak. Little Elisabetta peeks around the corner from the kitchen, wondering what is going on.

"My boss," says Rosina. "He saw me at my worktable this morning. I tried not to look at him, but I felt his eyes on me. He came behind me, standing very close, looking over my shoulder as if he is inspecting my work.

"I was sewing a ribbon on a hat. The way the girls work, all bunched together, makes it easy for the boss man. We are separate from the men. Unprotected. While the girls were all sewing buckles and ribbons and lace on the hats, the men are operating the machines, pressing the hats onto hot metal forms. They can't even see us.

"The boss man always likes to come by the girls and brush his thigh against us as he walks by. We get used to that. But today, he was too close. He stopped behind me. I felt his breath on the back of my neck. He started to push his body against mine."

"The monster!"

"But then he surprised me. He put both his hands on my shoulders. I tried to ignore him, but he slid his hands down toward my chest."

"So then I remember what you said, *Zia*—I use the hatpin. I don't even turn around. I held it like a knife and shoved it backwards. I stuck it right in his thigh."

"Brava! Good girl!"

"But that only made him mad! He shouted, said bad words. He told me to go to his office where he would deal with me. So I go. I watched boss man hurry to the washroom. Maybe he went to clean his wound. He held his thigh like it really hurt. I think he still had the pin stuck in him."

"I waited for him in his office. I was so scared, I started to cry. I didn't know what he was going to do. I waited a long time.

"Then I heard the door shut. He came at me and grabbed me by the arm, pushed me against the wall. He said no guinea wop was going to get away with what I did. He said what I did is a crime. He called it assault. He showed me the pin, said he will keep it, for evidence. He pinned it to his lapel. He said he'll tell the police I assaulted him. Me! He says I will go to jail!"

"He wouldn't dare!" I say. "You think he will admit to the police he was attacked by a little girl like you? Never."

"He said he will wear the pin now all the time, on his lapel where I can see it, to remind me he has power over me, to get me in trouble. But then he said, now I going to pay. He said he know about girls like me, Italian girls, peasants. How we like to do it on farms, like animals. I can't tell you all the things he said, filthy, filthy things."

"Rosina. Tell me. What did he do?"

"He pushed me down onto the floor. He was on top of me, so heavy. I tried to fight, couldn't breathe. He told me he knows how I like it. I am a whore, he said. He pushed up my skirt and tried to open his pants, but he couldn't do it with one hand. When he used both hands to open his pants, I saw my chance and ran away."

"But where was Giovanni all this time? The one with the thick neck?"

"You mean Giuseppe?" Rosina says. "His name is not Giovanni. It's Giuseppe! The girls told me he got fired yesterday after what he do to help me. They said he disrespected the boss."

Baby Girolamo is starting to fidget at my breast, and I have no patience with a little man interrupting me at a time like this.

"Hush, you little big mouth. Can't you see I'm busy? Rosina, let me put him in his crib and get you some tea. Elisabetta! Come rock your brother while I make tea."

When I come back to Rosina with a cup of tea in each hand, the girl is still shaking and sobbing. But I am no longer upset. I feel a sense of complete calm.

The solution is clear. Everything is going to be fine.

"Here, drink this nice hot tea. Yes, that's it, drink. You stay here for a while and rest. You don't go back to that place, ever. You get your strength back, you feel better. Nothing to worry about. You will get other jobs. Lots of other jobs."

"But he has the hatpin," Rosina says. "He will go to the police, tell them what happened."

"Don't you worry about that. I won't let him hurt you. But first, Rosina, you must tell me everything about this boss man. When he comes to work. When he goes home. You tell me everything.

"And that big strong man, Giuseppe. I need to find out where he lives, too."

———————

It is a week later. Stefano is reading the morning news at the head of the kitchen table, quietly sipping his coffee. I am rolling out pasta dough on the other end of the table to make linguine. I roll and roll the dough, stretching it further and further until it is paper thin, the way Albina showed me. Then I cut the pasta into smaller sheets and use my sharp knife and a ruler to slice the sheet into long thin ribbons.

"Celestina, did you see this? This story—I think this was Rosina's boss. He was hurt bad, right outside the Carroll Hixon factory. They say he was attacked, maybe sneak attack from behind. Someone beat him with a stick or a baseball bat. Smashed the back of his head. He lives, but he's hurt really bad. They don't think he'll ever be right in the head. They never found the weapon."

"*Peccato*," I say, without meaning it. I start laying the pasta ribbons to dry over a broomstick that I have balanced between the backs of two kitchen chairs.

"Good thing Rosina don't work there no more," Stefano says, flipping the newspaper to the next page. "That area not a safe place for a young girl."

"Rosina will be just fine," I say. "Lots of good jobs at the Milford Shoe."

I gather up all the loose scraps of pasta and form them into a ball and start rolling it out to make a new sheet.

Stefano looks up from his newspaper. That's when he notices my hands, rolling out the pasta dough.

"Why are you using a wine bottle to roll your pasta? What happen to your nice wooden rolling pin? The one I make for you?"

"Stefano. I… I don't have it no more. I burn it in the stove."

"What? Why you have to burn a rolling pin?"

"I was… I was in the cellar. I see a mouse. No, not a mouse. A rat. It was a big rat. I go get my rolling pin. I go to kill it with the rolling pin. I take a swing. Whack! Whack! Whack! Chase it all over the cellar. One time, I whack hard, and I don't miss. I get blood all over my rolling pin. Now it's no good. I use it for firewood."

"*Madonna mia!* What strength you have! Don't worry. I will make you another one."

Stefano goes back to reading his paper. "Looks like turkey selling for twenty-five cents a pound," he mumbles.

"Crazy," I say. "You can get lamb for half that."

"I don't eat lamb, you know that. Don't you ever buy the meat of a lamb!"

"I know, I know," I say, throwing my hands into the air. "You don't eat lamb. You say that a hundred times."

My husband folds up the newspaper and sets it aside as he rises to leave.

"And Celestina. What about the rat? You bury him?"

I look blankly at my husband and gather up my apron to wipe my hands.

"Yes, Stefano. That rat won't bother us anymore."

"Good girl." He nods in approval. I watch him reach for his Alpine hat and leave the house.

My Rosina silently walks up from the hall and stands in the kitchen doorway. I think she has been listening there the whole time. She stops and looks straight into my eyes.

She is fingering the head of the pin that fastens the front of her shawl. It is a bronze carnation.

Stefano, 1910

"Eh, *giovanotto…* you must be Marchigiano. You're wearing the Marchigiano shoes."

The young man stops in his tracks. He is taking a Sunday afternoon walk down Hayward Street and pauses to look down at his shoes. Then he looks up at me with puzzled eyes. I am standing behind my border wall, adding some cement and new stones, each one the size of an ostrich egg. It is now nearly three feet high. I stop to rub the gritty cement from my hands onto my pants and extend my hand over the wall.

"I am Stefano Marenghi," I say as he reaches out to shake my hand.

"I am Ferdinando Sacco. Why do you say I am Marchigiano?"

"Your shoes. All the Marchigiano men work in the iron foundry, and they all wear loafers like that, no shoelaces, so they can take them off quick when the hot iron spills on their feet. I know. I have worked there, too."

His face begins to soften into a smile. He looks young enough to be my son, skin smooth as a baby's, with a deep dimple crease in his cheeks when he smiles.

"I am not from the Le Marche. I am from Casalvecchio, in Foggia. I arrive in March of this year. I work in the foundry, yes, but only for a little while. Terrible work, like the fires of hell. I don't stay there long. Now I work at the Milford Shoe Company. I learn to make men's shoes."

His dialect is very strange. I don't understand every word he says. So I talk in slow, simple words to explain where I was born. I reach down to my foot to demonstrate where I come from.

"Italy is like a boot, no? This part of my leg is Italy. You're from the back of the ankle, down here, and I come from up here, on the knee." This makes him laugh.

"Me from the ankle, you from the knee!" he repeats. "I never hear anything so funny."

From that time on, I notice him more. I see him pass by most Sunday mornings and afternoons, sometimes walking alone, a young man lost in thought, as if he is pondering the great problems of the world. Sometimes I see him helping the older Italian ladies walk to church or to the market, arm in arm, patiently supporting them with the strength of his youth.

I want to know more about this young man, so I ask my neighbors. *Who is this Ferdinando, so often alone, looking so serious, seeming to carry such a heavy weight on his young shoulders?* I learn he is living just around the corner from me, boarding with the Calzone family on Mount Pleasant Street. He always waves when he walks by, sometimes lifting his foot and grabbing the back of his ankle with a big grin on his face. I lift my leg and grab my knee with both hands in reply.

One day, I ask him to join me for a glass of wine.

By now, my grape arbor in the back of the house has become well established, with thick twisting vines and abundant broad leaves, and it makes a nice shade from the sun. I offer him a sweet purple wine that I make with my own wine press. I pour two jiggers, and we sit on old wicker chairs, taking in the last sweet breath of summer.

"My father, in the Old Country, he was an olive oil merchant, but we had vineyards, also, with dark red grapes like these, Stefano. It's good to see a little piece of Italy here," he says.

It is the first of many talks under my grape arbor, always in a mix of Italian and English. Despite our different dialects, somehow, we find a way to understand each other. He tells me he came to America with his brother, Sabino. I tell him I, too, had traveled here with my brother. His family called him Nando from the time he was a boy, and with his permission, I now call him Nando, too.

I know the man has a tender heart because he tells me he can't stand it when one of the neighbors is butchering pigs or wringing a chicken's neck in the backyard. That's when he likes to sneak away and go for one of his long walks. He can't take the sight or sound of anything being killed. He says he could never kill an animal himself.

"I know how you feel, Nando. I once had a little lamb when I was a boy in Italy. I called her Angelina because she was a little angel. So pretty with her big eyes and her soft fur that curled around my fingers. My mamma, she think her little lamb is just like money in the bank, worth no more than a few *soldi* in her hand. Something to pay the doctor if we need one."

I tell Nando I was playing with my lamb in the snow when I slipped and fell, and my Angelina got away.

Nando smiles, but the memory makes my mood darken. I don't tell him the most important part of the story, how the lamb was killed because of my clumsiness on an icy bridge. And it was also the day my father died. That is too much death to share in one story. Maybe a story to save for later. Nando looks at me with eyes that seem to understand my sadness.

Little by little, I tell Nando more about my family. I tell him about my brother Pietro, and how he ships his daughters one by one to America —first Albina, then Rosina.

"Pietro thinks his girls have a better chance in America," I explain.

"That because all the young Italian men come here," Nando says.

I tell Nando that Pietro's girls are a big help taking care of my children. I tell him I have two sons, Bartolomeo and Girolamo, and little Elisabetta. We need help with the babies more than ever because Celestina helps me with my farming, too. Celestina even works at other people's farms when the season is right, like the cranberry farms in Holliston, and sometimes at flower farms. And there is always cleaning and cooking to do. So much women's work to be done. Rosina picks up where Albina left off, helping my Celestina.

When Nando comes to visit, I can sometimes see Rosina peering through the lace curtains to watch us sipping wine under the grape arbor. I think my niece might be taking a shine to my handsome young friend, with his strong cleft chin and sad gray eyes. Rosina and Nando are the same age, and they both work at the Milford Shoe factory.

One afternoon, she comes out to offer us a plate of biscotti to dip into our wine. I notice she has smoothed her dark hair with shiny pomade and put on a clean apron before stepping outside. "*Buona sera, Ferdinando,*" she says in barely a whisper. I see the way she avoids looking at him, keeping her eyes down to stop herself from blushing.

It is the fall of 1911, and Rosina and Ferdinando are both nineteen. I begin to think I would like to have this hard-working boy as my son-in-law. So I ask my wife Celestina what she thinks of the match. She is holding our newborn baby Cesarina, our fourth child, in one arm, adding wood to the big kitchen stove with the other. She does not hesitate to answer.

"I don't like that boy," she grumbles. "*Bass'italiano.* He will be nothing but heartbreak for her. He makes trouble, trying to make the men at the factory join his secret societies, his *socialisti.*"

I know what Celestina is talking about. Nando has been telling me lately about meetings he goes to with men who have strong ideas about politics. He likes to talk about how bad the rich men are. The big bosses, the captains of industry. How they make life hard for the working man. He uses words like socialists, anarchists. I don't know the difference. Most of the time, I don't think much about it.

"Celestina, you don't know him. Nando is a good boy."

"And why a Foggiano? Why can't she find a nice boy from our region, like Albina did? That way, if he decides to go back to the Old Country someday, they will both want to go to the same place."

"Maybe they will want to stay here."

"Stefano, you are too soft in the heart. Soft in the head, too. It makes you blind to people's faults."

"Celestina—"

"I understand that boy more than you do. He wants to rock the boat, wave his picket signs and flags. We are Italians here. We have to know our place, Stefano, behave like good *cittadini*, or they send us back to *la miseria* in the Old Country. We have to think about our good name."

At this moment, I hear steps running away, and through the window, I can see a glimpse of Rosina running outside toward the grape arbor. I follow her outside, but she keeps her back to me as she leans on one of the strong support poles of the arbor.

"Rosina, what's wrong? Tell your *Zio* Stefano."

"I hear you talking, and I know what *Zia* Celestina say is true. It's all true. Ferdinando comes to the shop sometimes in the morning and waits for me when I go to work. He tries to give me newspapers with bad names—*Il Proletario, Cronaca Sovversiva*—but I tell him no. I lie. I say I cannot read. His words scare me, *Zio*."

"But you like him, no?"

"I don't know what to think. I see him talk to you out here, so polite, so gentle, a good hard-working man, and I see how he is kind to the old women and to children. But he has ideas that I don't know. I don't understand them. I know they are dangerous ideas because he always whispers when he speaks of them, looks over his shoulder to see who is listening."

"Rosina, ever since your father sent you here, I try to be to be like a father to you. I want you to find a good man and be married. You're a pretty girl. You can marry any man you want, as long as you keep your eyes open and not go with someone who won't take care of you.

Your father would be very sorry to see you come all this way and be in a worse condition."

The next time I see my young friend, I ask him to sit with me and tell me about his newspapers.

"Nando, my niece—she tells me you give her newspapers. What newspapers you give her?"

Nando reaches into his jacket and pulls out a rolled-up newspaper.

"Yes, I will show you. I have an article that I wrote in this one…" He pauses when he sees the blank expression on my face and puts the paper back inside his jacket.

"Never mind the newspaper. I will tell you, Stefano. When your family and mine come to this country, we think America will embrace us like a mother, welcome us, give us honest labor, no? But we are given the worst jobs. Look at the work Italians do—pouring melted iron in the foundry. Hot, dangerous work. Or cutting stone at the quarries, breathing in that dust that makes them sick in the lungs.

"The very worst jobs go to Italians, Stefano. The worst! And that General Draper, Mr. Bigshot, owns the biggest factory around. They build a statue of him, high and mighty on his horse in Draper Park. They cover him in medals and make statues, while his family lines their pockets with gold. All of it built on the backs of the Italians!"

"Nando, be careful of your words. The Draper family is rich and powerful."

"And you will defend them, Stefano? You will defend the rich boss? Who will speak for the worker, the one who breaks his back to bring home a few pennies for his family? Why do you not cry for the workers? I tell you, Stefano, we do not live in America. We live *under* America. Under it. So far under it we cannot breathe."

I don't know what to think. I feel so much affection for the boy. I would proudly call him my son. But he has big ideas that are too big for me to understand. In Italy, I would never have a house like this, or land of my own, or this grape arbor that shades my face from the sun. What causes such passion to burn in Nando's young heart?

Celestina, 1911

I tell my Rosina that she has a letter from Pereto. She has been washing the dishes in my kitchen sink and stops and wipes her hands on her apron. The letter is from her mother, Amalia. I watch her tear the envelope and carefully unfold the onionskin letter.

"Read it to me, Rosina!"

She hesitates, wants to feel the words penned by her mamma, take them in slowly, like gentle whispers in her ear. Finally, she sits at the table and reads:

> *Your letter arrived, and we were so happy. We still can't believe you are so far away, and now four years have gone by. You were so brave to have made that long voyage all alone.*
>
> *Can you believe your sister Tranquilla is sixteen? And Uggero is now working with his father, learning to be a stonemason. He is a man now. You would not recognize him, big shoulders and taller than his father. And Mario and Florinda are getting taller every day. All of my children grow faster than the summer corn.*
>
> *When we got your last letter, we told your friend Pina. She wants to hear more about your handsome friend—*

At this, my little niece stops reading and starts to blush. I know her mother is asking about Ferdinando. Rosina does not want to speak his name. She turns the page and picks up reading again.

> *Pina has already turned down five suitors. So fussy! And men are so precious and few in our village. Now the only one left is the hunchback. Do you remember him? Twice her age. And can you believe it? Pina says she will marry him!*

Please send the package as soon as you can. I am glad you are able to find good cloth in America. Many people are coming for Pina's wedding in March, and some cloth for new clothes will be just in time. Tranquilla will be a bridesmaid.

Thank you for sending the ribbons and combs. Maybe you can send food, too? My friend Irena is sick with the pellagra. She has the rash around her neck, the Casal necklace. She is tired and sleeps all day. We all went to visit her, and we said our rosary.

The doctor says she needs different food. She eats only corn. Maybe you can send cans of sardines, tuna, the kind of food that will survive the long voyage? Enough to share with Irena?

Pina is always discussing how you made a mistake by shipping yourself over there. Maybe she is just jealous. Or maybe she misses her old friend and wants you here. I tell her you will want to return to see your dear homeland again, as well as your friends and your family who love you very much. And you will have a husband at your side and a baby in your lap.

The sheep, the goats, the piglets, and even the hedgehog want to say they miss you. We shed many tears each night when we think of you. Your letters are a treasure, but I want to see you, my daughter, my flesh and bone!

I wish I were a butterfly so I could fly across the ocean to you."

At this, Rosina stops reading, her voice starting to break as a tear runs down her cheek. She turns away, not wanting me to see her face. I know she misses her mamma. I see her fold the precious letter, return it to the envelope, and stuff it inside her blouse. I wonder if there is more, but I don't want to ask.

"That's all she writes, *Zia* Celestina."

I tell her not to worry. We will fill a big box with clothes and food and send it to her mother.

"I will write another letter, *Zia*, to put in the box you send. I want to give my love to my friend Pina. Maybe she will be happy with the hunchback. At least he won't be chasing after other women."

That Rosina makes me laugh sometimes.

"And Rosina, don't forget when you write your letter to give your love to the sheep and the goats and the pigs, and the hedgehog, too."

———————

Again, my nipples are sore and red, another baby at my breast. Little Rosina tries to be a help, but she cannot put my little Cesarina to her breast. She can only help cook and clean and wash clothes for my Bartolomeo, Elisabetta, and Girolamo.

Today she lays out four bowls of steaming soup for me and the children and slices the crusty bread on the wooden breadboard. A little piece of bread is placed by each bowl. Then she calls my little ones to the kitchen for lunch. She is such a picture of sweetness. Does she have any thoughts in her head besides her work, her daily bread, and a warm place to sleep at night? Does she ever think dark thoughts about her old boss man, the one with lust like a wolf? I think she is a simple girl, and that's all for the best.

As for me, I learned a long time ago to put my thoughts into little drawers in my mind and store them away until I need them. I don't need to think about that boss man; his ugly deeds will stay hidden and unspoken forever. I will shed no tears for him.

Rosina finally fills a bowl for herself. She carefully lowers herself onto a wooden chair with a heavy sigh, as if that chair was the softest feather bed. That's how happy she is to finally sit down.

"Rosina, I want to talk to you."

She looks up warily from her soup.

"Please, eat your soup. Don't let it get cold. Eat."

I dip the bread in my soup and eagerly bring it to my mouth while Rosina sips her soup cautiously. She is wary of what I am going to say.

"Rosina, you are nineteen years old. When I was your age, I already had a husband and two little ones. You think about marriage, no?"

She shakes her head without looking at me.

"Is that dark Foggiano still in your thoughts?"

"You mean Ferdinando? No, *Zia*, no. I don't think about him. He is not for me. He spends his time with radicals, the ones who give all us Italians a bad name. They meet in dark corners."

"Yes, I know. Their numbers are growing in our town."

"I remember, *Zia*. There was a story in the newspaper, not long ago, a strike in the town of Lawrence. The girls in the shop were talking about it. The textile workers went marching in the streets. Same kind of workers we have in our town. People filling every corner of the street. They make a lot of noise, wave their picket signs. Men hitting each other with picket signs, like animals. Women and children marching, too."

"Yes, I remember. People firing guns. Someone got killed. A woman, I think."

"Yes. Many people arrested. I remember this story because one of them was a friend of Nando's, Arturo Giovanitti. He writes for *Il Proletario,* one of Nando's favorites. I hear Arturo is a troublemaker. They say he makes speeches that set people's hearts on fire. He talks about how the gun shops are going to be busy. He tells the strikers to prowl around like wild animals, looking for the blood of the scabs. That's what the girls at the shop tell me."

"They arrest him, Rosina, this Arturo?"

"Yes! He started a riot where someone got killed. He can go to jail for that! I am afraid there are more troubles to come. I hear people say this strike in Lawrence is just the beginning. It is going to spread to all the factory towns. Milford will be next. I know it. I don't want trouble, but I feel it coming. It makes me afraid."

"So, Rosina, what does Ferdinando do? He joins the strikers?"

"Oh, *Zia*. If he were smart, he would shut his mouth, go to work every day, and mind his own business. Instead he is raising money for his friend Arturo, helping him get a lawyer. Everyone knows about it. He makes no secrets. He helps these dangerous men when he should be staying far away. He puts on little plays in our neighborhood and sells tickets to raise money. Everyone knows."

"You know, Rosina, I tell Stefano all the time he needs to stay away from that Ferdinando. He is going to be in jail someday, maybe worse. That's not good for our family, to be seen with someone like that. I try to tell him to think about our reputation."

"I know, *Zia*, I know. For me, I just want a nice hard-working man. I want to raise a family. I don't want any trouble. I want you and *Zio* Stefano to come to see me in my own house someday—a nice house, with a good man, and babies in my arms. A simple life. Not crying for a foolish man who is wasting his life in jail."

Baby Cesarina starts fidgeting, and I shift her from one breast to the other. With my free hand, I continue dipping my bread into my broth and feeding myself. Crumbs and drippings spill onto the bib of my apron, but I don't care.

"More bread, Rosina!" She hands me the heel of the loaf, which I tear in two with my teeth and dip the raw edge into my soup bowl. Nursing babes always makes me hungry. Without having to be asked, Rosina is rounding up the three children, seven, six, and five years old, and leads them away for a nap. When she returns, she starts clearing the plates.

I don't know what I'd do without her.

"Rosina," I say, with a full mouth, "what about that big strong man, Giovanni?"

"You mean Giuseppe? The man who protected me? I see him sometimes hanging around Milford Shoe when I leave work. I think he's keeping an eye on me. But if he sees me talking to Nando, he goes away."

"You never speak to this Giuseppe?"

"No, he doesn't come close."

"You could do worse than Giuseppe. A lot worse. Maybe you should encourage him a little bit. Here, take Cesarina. I need to go lie down for a while."

What a relief to leave my four children in this girl's care. I need to get a little rest, too. I think I will keep planting Giuseppe's name in her head, like a seed that will slowly grow. It might take her a long time to warm up to him and erase Nando completely from her mind. Until then, I will keep her busy. I will need her capable hands and strong young back.

Stefano, 1912

I had my big hopes that Nando would marry my niece, and then I could call him my son. I would be proud to have him in my family.

But somehow, Rosina has met a much older man, Giuseppe Tolenti. A good solid type with skin as brown as a chestnut from working outside in the sun. She is twenty years old now, the same age as Nando, and her new suitor Giuseppe is thirty-five. I thought he was too old for her, but I can't say anything about that. I was sixteen years older than Celestina when I married her.

Celestina is all in favor of the match. I can't figure out why. My wife seems connected to this man by some force I cannot explain. She says to me, "This man will protect our Rosina. He won't let anything happen to her. He will go to the ends of the earth for her." I don't know why she is so sure about that.

Rosina and Giuseppe become man and wife in October 1912, and just one month later, my friend Nando marries a pretty red-haired girl named Rosa Zambelli.

Before long, my niece and Giuseppe are blessed with their first baby, a beautiful boy, Alessandro. The family has a house on the north side of town, on West Street. It's not far from Giuseppe's new job at the Draper factory just over the Milford border in Hopedale. Giuseppe is a molder in the iron foundry, putting his good solid back to work. Rosina stays home with her baby but does some piecework from her house, sewing buckles and buttons on shoes when her baby is sleeping.

We don't see Rosina anymore except on Sundays, when she and her husband and baby come for Sunday dinner. On one of these Sunday dinners, I ask Giuseppe why they don't live in Hopedale. Such a quiet and pretty little town. But he tells me Italians are not allowed to live there.

"We're good enough to work in the foundry but not good enough to live in the same town as the almighty Draper family," he tells me.

"How you know this, Giuseppe?"

"You can ask my friend, Guido Mazzarelli, the one who makes the good bread we are eating."

"Yes, this is bread from his bakery on Genoa Avenue."

"Well, Guido isn't allowed to drive his carriage through Hopedale to make his deliveries. He has to take the rough back roads around Hopedale, miles out of his way, to get his bread to the next town."

"But how do they know he's Italian?"

"Stefano! His name is painted on the side of his carriage!" Celestina interrupts. She holds her hands up in the air in exasperation, as if asking the Lord for strength.

"Yes," Giuseppe adds with a smile. "That's true. But even if he paints a different name, they know who we are. They always know who we are. I walk to work every morning, and at night, I go straight home. I don't stick around. I know I am not welcome there after sundown."

Giuseppe reminds me of Nando when he talks this way. He has a little of Nando's passion, some fire in his eyes when he speaks.

Meanwhile, I continue to see my friend Nando whenever I can. When I see him and his new wife walking arm in arm together, I like to take off my felt hat, compliment Rosa on her pretty red hair, and take a deep bow to show off my own hair of the same color.

"Maybe your pretty redhaired bride is my cousin, Nando!" I like to make him laugh. Such a serious face all the time. He needs to smile once in a while.

I always want to invite the young couple to my house and drink wine the way Nando and I used to do, but my Celestina does not approve. I wish she wouldn't hate him so much. He's such a nice boy.

"He gives Italians a bad name!" my wife complains to me. "He's a bomb thrower. He makes people think all Italians are bomb throwers."

"He's not a bomb thrower! Nando never hurt anybody!"

"He will! If he hasn't thrown a bomb already, he will!"

"Okay, okay, maybe we don't invite them into our house. But maybe we can go see one of his plays?"

"What plays? Plays about bomb throwers?"

"I don't know. One of them is called 'Rassapoot.' Or maybe 'Rassaputin. Rasspoopin.' Something like that. Maybe it's a play about cowboys, like all the shoot-em-up movies these days. You know, the ones about the pioneers in the covered wagons."

"I'll tell you about pioneers! The Italians! We're the pioneers! Stupid covered wagons, people getting plenty of nice fresh air and sunshine, go to California. Let them try traveling 5,000 miles in a stinking ship, see how they like it."

O dio mio.

But I miss my friend Nando. I feel in my heart he is a good man, a tender-hearted man, and he will forget someday the radical ways of his youth. These are the passions of young men. As he gets older, wiser, he will think more about his family and not worry about other people's problems.

I keep pressing my Celestina to invite Ferdinando and his bride Rosa to our house. She is sick of hearing me ask, so she finally gives in.

"Just one time!" she says. "Just once!"

My hope is she will change her mind when she sits down with him, breaks bread with them. She will see he is a good person, just like us.

It's a Saturday afternoon. I have been whistling all day and feeling a lightness in my step, all because Ferdinando and Rosa will be coming to have supper with us tonight. My Celestina has been busy cooking all day, making her good potato pie, rolling pasta for ravioli, and simmering an aromatic chicken broth on the stove. There is a plate of our own sweet sausages on the table, pink and shiny, ready to be fried until crisp and brown. A dozen fresh peaches have been washed and are draining in a colander by the sink. They will be sliced and dipped in glasses of red wine for dessert. Little Elisabetta, just seven years old, is helping her mother with the cooking, using a little spoon to fill the pasta. She is learning. Mother and daughter are covered with flour.

Later, when the kitchen is clean and the children freshly washed, I hear our guests arrive. I leap up and run to the door.

"Look, Celestina! The young bride and groom are here! *Benvenuti*, Nando, Rosa, come, come in, come into our kitchen!"

I tell Bartolomeo to take Rosa's coat and hat, like a good boy, and then I show the honored guests to our table. Rosa offers to help Celestina with the cooking, but my wife refuses, telling her guest to sit. I think my talkative Celestina is being a little too quiet tonight, turning her back to our guests while she cooks.

Rosa instead takes the children out to the parlor to tell them a story while I fill two jiggers with my own sweet purple wine. I clink glasses with Nando, and he takes a seat at the table, complimenting Celestina for the fine aromas that fill the room.

My wife says nothing.

"Look, Nando, look at the solid legs on this table. I make it myself, the strongest oak. And just look at this tablecloth—Celestina made this."

I hold up the edge of the cream-colored cloth, revealing the tightly woven loops, chains, and open work that form a veil of the tiniest leaves and flowers over my hands.

"See, the lace tatting. Celestina does this work herself."

"It is very fine, Stefano. Very fine."

I am bursting with pride when the food is all laid on the table in great steaming bowls. I don't think there is a finer cook in Milford. We like to show *abbondanza*—abundance—when guests are in the house. No matter how poor we are or how little we have, we must show great generosity to our guests.

Four adults and my four children gather around our table. Our mixed Italian dialects blend like a strange new spice sprinkled over our food. The sounds of children loudly slurping their broth add to the symphony. Through it all, Celestina is silent. I try to engage her in conversation with our guests.

"Doesn't Rosa have pretty red hair, Celestina? Just like all the women who come from my village in the Old Country, no?

Celestina ignores the question and speaks directly to Nando. Her sudden directness is surprising and intense.

"Are you still working at the Milford Shoe? Our niece Rosina used to see you there."

Her eyes never leave Nando's face.

"Yes, Celestina. I still work there."

"She says you always have newspapers, written in Italian."

"I try to share my newspapers, yes, with people I know and trust."

"I prefer to read the newspapers in English, like the *Milford Daily News*. It's good to learn the language when you live in America, this great country that gives us work and bread and wine, and a roof over our heads. Don't you think so?"

Now I worry. I see my wife as a cunning archer, quietly drawing back the arrow in her bow. I am afraid of what force she will release when she is finally ready to strike.

"*Signora*, I think this country was made by good men with great ideas. This country makes big promises to its people. I don't think it always keeps its promises. Maybe to some but not to everyone."

"You seem to do well here. You learn a new trade, you make shoes, you make a good living. You can afford a wife who likes to wear pretty dresses and hats, and I think you have food on your table. You don't look like a man who is starving."

The atmosphere is growing tense, and I squirm in my chair. "Celestina," I say softly, "I think we need more bread on the table. Can you bring us some more bread, *per favore?*"

Without leaving her chair, Celestina reaches sideways to the cupboard beside her and pulls another loaf from the breadbox, her eyes fixed the whole time on Nando. Ignoring the knife on the cutting board, she tears the loaf violently into rough pieces, letting them fall on the breadboard. I think she would like to tear Nando to bits with her bare hands.

"I tell you what I think," Celestina announces, with a little more volume in her voice. "I never had a table with food like this when I lived in Varsi. Here, we eat. We eat good. I think when a country is good to you, you say 'thank you.' You don't bite the hand that feeds you."

Nando stiffens upright in his chair. I don't think a woman has ever spoken to him this way before.

Suddenly, Rosa makes a surprising declaration.

"Nutmeg!"

All eyes turn to her. She is smiling sweetly while holding the soup spoon to her mouth.

"Yes, I can taste it. My mother put nutmeg in her ravioli, too."

"You know this recipe?" My wife looks astonished. The pretty Rosa with flaming hair, the one she has been ignoring ever since she arrived, is now speaking a language my wife understands. The language of cooking.

"And if I am not mistaken, Celestina, you have put a little lemon juice in your chicken broth."

"Yes, yes! I did! It cuts the oily taste."

"But where do you find lemons? None of the grocers have them."

"My husband. He goes to Haymarket Square in Boston. Don't you, Stefano?"

I feel a rush of joy at this sudden turn in the conversation and join in.

"Yes, I do! Yes! I go to Haymarket sometimes. I buy muscat grapes when I don't have enough for my wine, and for this special dinner, my wife tells me to get lemons. And look—just look at these peaches!"

I reach for the bowl that Celestina has covered with a dishcloth to keep the flies away. With great flourish, I whip off the cloth to reveal the perfect golden peach slices edged with dark red at the core, glistening in their own juice.

"I bought them from the pushcart vendors a few days ago. They are just perfect now, ripe and sweet."

"We will dip them in red wine later," Celestina explains.

"Oh, Celestina, Nando and I like nothing better than fresh peaches in red wine. You must come to our house sometime. I will give you some of my almond biscotti, and we will dip those in red wine, too."

Nando looks at me, and I see his stiff posture has softened. He draws his index finger to his lips, as if to say, "Be silent. The women have taken over the conversation. Let us be happy to savor our food in peace."

Later that night, sitting under the grape arbor with no other illumination but the light that spills from the kitchen windows, Nando and I watch the animated movements of our wives as they clear the table. We see only the women's shoulders and heads through the windows as they move about the kitchen.

I click my wine glass to Nando's and raise it to make a toast.

"Welcome to my home, Nando. Welcome."

Stefano, 1913

As we come marching, marching, we battle too for men,
For they are women's children, and we mother them again.
Our lives shall not be sweated from birth until life closes;
Hearts starve as well as bodies; give us bread, but give us roses!

—*James Oppenheim*

I am worried. Milford is starting to see the kind of strikes and rabble-rousing that made headlines in Lowell and Lawrence. Even the mighty Draper Company in Hopedale is starting to see picket signs. No one ever thought it would happen there. The newspapers always say Draper is good to its workers, and happy workers don't go on strike. I guess they don't ask the Italians in the foundry how they feel about it. They just ask the ones who work in comfortable leather chairs all day.

I'm glad I don't work at Draper anymore. I'm happy with my hoe and my plow, working my own land, not having to talk to anybody but my horse most of the time.

I know a little about what's going on. I read the *Milford Daily News* every day because it helps me pick up a few more words of English here and there. Besides what I read in the paper, I can always count on getting the news from the Italian women who live up and down the street and share the latest news over clotheslines and kitchen tables. They know whatever the newspapers omit. Sometimes the newspapers don't like to tell the whole story and pretend nothing is happening. I think they don't want to offend the Draper family.

But we always know what's going on.

From what I hear and what I read, more than a thousand men, mostly immigrants, gathered on April 1 to block the workers from entering the foundry at Draper. They had help from a labor union that came all the way from Chicago. This is a different kind of labor union that takes all kinds of workers, skilled and unskilled, women and men— even the unemployed. Immigrants, too. No unions ever wanted immigrants before. People call this union the Wobblies—I don't know why. They come halfway across the country just to organize the strikers in the little town of Hopedale.

The Wobblies know how to organize, and not just the Draper workers. The cigar makers and the granite worker unions are also joining in solidarity. The strikers are growing and growing in numbers, not just here but all over the country. Lately, the Wobblies are going back and forth between here and New Jersey to mobilize the silk workers. I hear lots of Italians work there, too.

Every day, I think more and more that Nando was right. He said Italians are not living *in* America but *under* America, and nothing will change until we make a lot of noise. But who has the courage to make noise when our jobs can so easily be taken from us?

I know Nando, for one, is not afraid. The more he is busy with the strikers, the less I see him. Sometimes I ask my *compare* what they hear about him, and I can see they are sometimes afraid to speak. So many of my Italian friends don't want to stir the pot or be seen as trouble-makers. They whisper when they tell me about Nando.

They tell me he is getting mixed up with two different radical groups— one on Plains Street, one on East Main. They have about fifty members, most of them countrymen of his, the Foggianos. Even Celestina knows about this. She often goes to Nando's house to see her new friend Rosa, and when she comes home, I ask what she hears about Nando. Celestina tells me what I already know. Nando is standing in picket lines at Draper, even though he doesn't work there anymore, to support the workers and their right to have a union.

Celestina also tells me that Nando and Rosa are expecting a baby. It makes me sad that Nando is not the one to tell me this happy news.

I don't understand why he takes risks with secret societies and picket lines when he has a pregnant young wife at home. I hope nothing will happen to him.

Meanwhile, Draper is making noise, too. I read it in the paper. Draper is standing firm and says that any man who joins the picket line will lose his job and his company housing, too. Eben Draper, the top man at the company, has lots of bigshot friends. He used to be the governor of Massachusetts. Twice, when he was governor, they asked him to sign a law to give the workers a shorter workday—eight hours a day. And twice he refused. He is not going to change his mind now.

An eight-hour day. That's what everyone wants. It doesn't seem so much to ask.

There's a song that some of the Italians sing when they are on strike outside of Draper. It's a catchy song. I hear people singing it on the streets and in their houses. They say it's the same song the *mondine* used to sing while marching on the streets of Italy to protest their long hours in the rice fields:

> *Se otto ore sembran poche*
> *Provate voi a lavorar*
> *e provarete la differenza*
> *di lavorare e comandar*

> If eight hours seem few to you
> Try working eight hours yourself
> And you'll see the difference
> Between working and giving orders

I wonder how many countries are feeling the roar of the workers singing and shouting? Like earthquakes rumbling all over the world. That's how it feels to me.

Even young women with babies in their arms, and children, too, are marching to support the strikes, parading through town, singing songs. Some of them sing a French song I've never heard before, the Marsay—Marsell—something like that. It is the French national anthem. I don't know where they get all these songs.

Every day, new threats, new troubles. I don't even want to open the newspaper anymore. One evening, I read about a streetcar traveling from Milford to Hopkinton, and just when they got to the turn-around, gunshots were fired. A Draper man, one of the higher-ups who worked in the nice clean office, a company man of twenty-five years, was hit with a bullet in the thigh. Four other passengers ducked just in time as bullets went flying through the walls of the bus and whizzing over their heads. It's lucky no one was killed.

Dio mio.

Every day, I see police, even in my own neighborhood, patrolling the streets. I don't like to see police walking around with guns. People say they are here to protect the streetcars from rock throwers, but I think they come to keep an eye on us Italians, to make sure we know our place. Our place under their feet.

Even the young girls working at Greene Brothers factory and the Lapworth Mill are starting to organize. They found out the men at Draper were on strike for more money, and those men were already getting fifteen dollars a week. Now these girls and women say they want more money, too. And why not? They don't even make five dollars a week. They say they want five dollars a week to start and ten dollars for the more experienced girls. That's all they are asking for.

Those women are as strong as the men, maybe stronger. One morning, a riot broke out among the strikers in front of the Lapworth Mill. It started when the boss, Frank Lapworth, tried to bring some new girls to the mill in his big car. The women in the picket line threw stones at the car, breaking the windows.

And then the riot broke out. Women were fighting with rocks, sticks, and even their umbrellas. The men were on strike, too, but most of them stood back and out of the way. I think they were afraid of the women with their pointed umbrellas. The newspaper said the women had torn their dresses and had blood on their faces.

They say they need to have one police officer on duty for every ten men on strike. I say they need to have *ten* policemen on hand for every *one* woman on strike. That's what I think.

When the Draper management tries to send replacement workers—scabs—on the trolley cars that run in the morning from Holliston to Milford to Hopedale, women rush onto the cars and bang pots and pans, yell insults at the scabs, and try to drag them off the trains. Picturing these fierce women armed with pots and pans reminds me of my Celestina, the way she gets when she gets fire in her eyes.

I'm glad my niece Rosina isn't working at the shoe factory anymore. Ever since she got married, she only does piecework at home. She is pregnant again and already lost one baby. My wife says he is having trouble with the pregnancy, too. She was always a delicate girl. The doctor tells her to stay in bed as much as she can.

I am also glad to be home, living my life as a peaceful farmer. I am feeding my family from the gardens around my house and selling what we can't eat to our neighbors. No matter what happens in the world, I will always be able to feed my family. I decided a long time ago that I don't want to rock the boat. On that, I agree with my Celestina.

But no one can ignore the trouble. You can feel it in the air, a poisonous wind, the breath of a viper about to strike. It gives me a feeling of dread in my stomach, every day, as if I had swallowed a heavy stone.

And every day I look for news of my friend Nando. I hope I don't see his name in the paper. I see nothing that mentions him by name, but I know he will always be there at Draper with the others, holding the picket signs, blocking the path where men enter the foundry, calling them scabs if they try to pass.

With all the special police forces that Draper has hired and hundreds of strikers blocking its doors every day, something is bound to happen. Someone will get hurt. I just know it.

Celestina, 1913

It's Thursday morning, April 24. Stefano and I are working the earth in our gardens, getting the beautiful black soil turned and ready for spring planting. My sister Maria is in the house watching Girolamo and Cesarina, while Bartolomeo and Elisabetta are off at school.

I look up for a moment to wipe the sweat from my face with my apron, and I am surprised to see one of the women from my street running to my neighbor's house and pounding on the door. After she shares her news with the lady of the house, we hear a shriek that raises the hair on my arms. It makes Stefano look up, too.

We see other women running from house to house like a human telephone line, their apron strings flying behind them as they spread their urgent news. I drop my hoe, walk toward the road, and call out to one of the women, a neighbor I recognize.

"Desolina! Desolina! *Che cosa c'è?*"

"Emilio Bacchiocchi! Assassinato, 'sta mattina, nello sciopero di Draper!"

What is this? Emilio? That nice young Marchigiano? Killed in the strike? No. Not Emilio. He is one of us! We know his family on Cedar Street. Just a short walk from here. Stefano knows him. Used to work with him. At Draper. He has a wife. Two young children.

I start feeling a tightness in my throat, a dryness. I cannot speak. This awful business with the strikes has now hit close to home.

I turn around to look for Stefano. I don't see him working outside anymore. Where did he go? Did he hear what Desolina said about Emilio? If he did, he would take the news hard. I need to find him quickly.

I run into the house looking for him. He's not in the kitchen, not in the parlor. I go to the stairs, and I see my little sister Maria running down the steps. She is upset, shaken by something.

"Come quick," she tells me, leading the way to the first little bedroom upstairs. I find Stefano on his knees, hugging Girolamo and Cesarina. Tears run down his face. He is sobbing like a baby. My little ones don't know what's going on. They look confused and frightened. Why is their father squeezing them so tight?

I go to kneel on the floor behind my husband and wrap my arms around him and my children.

"I know, Stefano," I whisper. "I know."

———————

In the late afternoon, my family is gathered in my kitchen. Our children are home from school. My parents have joined us, along with my sister Maria, my brother Giuseppe, and his wife Maria Malvermi. My niece Rosina and her husband Giuseppe are here. We have all read the afternoon paper, and we have heard what our neighbors have said and witnessed. The children are instinctively silent and still. They know something is wrong. We are all grieving as if we have lost one of our own sons.

Rosina and Giuseppe are the most upset. Giuseppe went to work at Draper this morning. He was there.

"I went in early, before seven," Giuseppe says. "I needed extra time to get through the picket lines. Emilio was close to the entrance, like always. He was looking at me when I went in to work. He was disapproving. I could see it in his eyes. But the armed guards—Draper has an army of them—they cleared a way for the workers like me to come in. They let us pass. Then when I was inside, I heard a loud roar. A horrible sound. Men shouting. It sounded like a fight. Then the shots. We all heard the shots."

"What happened, Giuseppe? The papers say Emilio was attacking the guard. They say he had a weapon," Luigi said.

"He did not have a weapon! None of the strikers did! Emilio would never bring a weapon. Never!" Giuseppe says. His voice is shaking.

"Yes," Stefano says. "That's the Emilio I know. Gentle, spoke softly. Never hurt anybody."

"The police say Emilio and the others were throwing stones. But it didn't happen that way!" says Giuseppe. His fist pounds the table. His voice is getting louder and angrier as he continues:

"The workers who were outside when it happened—they saw everything, and they came in to tell us. They say Emilio was running away when he was shot. The guard chased him like an animal and shot him in the back. How can he be a threat when he is running away? The police shot an innocent man in the back!"

Rosina placed her hand on her husband's arm to calm him. Giuseppe's eyes are red and full of tears.

"There will be a trial. So many witnesses saw what happened," my brother Giuseppe says. "The guard will be punished."

"You think so? You think they will believe the Italians? Or will they believe the guards who work for the Draper family?"

I don't want to think about that. Instead, I think about poor Emilio. Just an ordinary family man, not very different from my Stefano or any of the men in this room. In the blink of an eye, now he becomes a martyr. I think of his wife, too, and the help she will need. I will cook later tonight and bring her some food in the morning.

The next day, I go with my husband to Emilio's wake at the Edwards Funeral Home. This is the first time I've ever been to such a strange place. Most people I know lay out their coffins in their own homes, in parlors, or in their kitchens. But with so many people who want to pay their respects to Emilio's wife and family, Edwards is the only place big enough to hold them all.

I am surprised to see Nando standing outside the funeral home as we arrive. What is he doing? He is handing out postcards to the mourners who are coming to the wake. The card has a picture of two of Emilio's little boys, one of them still a toddler in long hair and a white dress. Both boys are now fatherless. He is urging people to give as much money as they can to support the grieving family.

Stefano seems to get a lift from seeing his old friend and gives Nando a long hug. He left the young man's shoulder wet with his tears.

On the day of Emilio's funeral, all the businesses in the Plains section of town are closed. The morning air is heavy with a cold, gray mist. You would think it was December, but it is only the last days of April.

Leaving the house, I am chilled by the total silence. The only sound is that of a single crow dressed all in black like a widow, cawing hoarsely from its perch in the branches of our cherry tree. A pair of crows would be a good omen, but a single crow means very bad luck to come.

I take Stefano by the arm to walk him slowly to the corner. There is not a single carriage or car on the streets. Stefano shuffles like an old man. I am holding his arm, supporting him, and not the other way around. He is forty-three years old, but I think he aged ten years that day. The two of us wait at the corner of Hayward Street and East Main until we see the approaching funeral procession.

At the head of the procession, a squad of young men on black bicycles, their handlebars draped with black ribbons. Then comes a group of girls on foot all dressed in white and holding white flowers, and then men with flowing black ribbon ties around their necks and black mourning badges on their arms. A pair of women carry a large oval portrait of Emilio and his wife, framed with white carnations. There are two bands in the parade. I think it must be the biggest funeral Milford has ever seen.

Soon, we see our friends and neighbors, many familiar faces, and many I've never seen before, marching in wide rows the width of the street. We wait until we see an opening and join the other marchers. We all solemnly walk together, many like Stefano and me, holding long-stemmed red carnations. We march up East Main Street, past all the houses with black crepe paper draped over the doors. No one speaks. When the music pauses, you can hear the sound of crepe paper fluttering in the wind. A sound I'll always remember.

We enter the Sacred Heart of Jesus Church where Father Petrarca says the funeral Mass. We are lucky to get a seat. Most of the mourners can't fit inside and strain to listen from outdoors.

After the Mass, another procession walks to the St. Mary's Cemetery. Emilio's body is carried away like a king in a gleaming black hearse pulled by four silver-gray horses, each one decorated with white ribbons and a plume on its head.

Behind the hearse, one of Emilio's little boys walks alone with a large sign that reads, "I am the son of the assassinated one."

―――――――――――

The rage against this injustice will not die quickly. One of our own has been killed.

In every corner of our town, you can feel it. Even the children at the Plains School arm themselves with clubs and stones to block children from entering the school, copying the strikers' behavior that they hear about from their parents. Police are called to break up a reported strike at the Plains School, and they are stunned to find that the strikers are only small children.

In these dark days, we all follow the newspapers closely. Strikers, mostly Italian, are arrested daily. But none of the special police officers are arrested. Even Nando's friend, Arturo Giovanitti, the one who caused so much trouble in Lawrence, is arrested here in Milford. More than once.

And the one who killed Emilio? I read about that in the paper, too. He went on trial, if you can call it that. This so-called policeman—the assassin—claims that shooting Emilio was justified. And at the end of the trial, the judge agrees. That is his verdict. The man who killed Emilio is found innocent.

But how can that be? He shoots a man in the back while he is running away. How is that justified? Is no one safe in the hands of Draper's hired guns, who can get away with murdering Italians like rabid dogs?

Three of Milford's Italian police officers resign in protest over the verdict. Officer Antonio de Pasquale is in the courtroom when they read the verdict. He threw down his badge to the floor and shouted, "You can give my badge to any officer who has the same idea of fair play as the one who committed this act."

There is no justice for the Italian worker. I can see that now. But I can't help worrying that Nando and Arturo, the Wobblies, and all their comrades will only make it worse. I am convinced of that. Nothing will change. By and by, all these strikes will be over, and we'll all be back where we started.

That's what I tell my Stefano, but he doesn't believe me. Not yet.

———————

Every day, the newspapers get harder and harder to read, heavy with so much bad news. Some new arrests, some new brawls and disturbances. Italians who risked their jobs for striking at Draper are now being kicked out of company housing in Prospect Heights, losing their jobs and their homes at the same time. Over one hundred families have to leave town to find work. Since Draper pays for its own police forces, loyal to Draper alone, anyone who goes on strike there is taking his life in his hands.

But those who don't go on strike are risking their lives, too. Any man suspected of being a Draper scab is clubbed and beaten on the streets by total strangers. I worry about Rosina because someone threw a rock through one of her windows. Do they think Giuseppe is a scab because he goes to work at Draper every day?

I don't know what choice he has. How can a factory worker choose between doing what is right for the workers and putting food in his children's mouths? An impossible choice.

If the sun has shone in the sky even once this year, I do not remember it.

Stefano, 1913

Enough. It's more than one man can take. I need to get away from the daily news, from the newspapers, from the women chattering with Celestina in our kitchen. But I have to be very careful. I don't want my wife to know where I'm going.

I quietly slip out of the house to go to Nando's. I can't wait to see his new baby boy. Celestina would erupt like Mount Vesuvius if she knew. She is angry again at Nando, but this time it is because he refuses to baptize his baby. But I won't be gone very long. Celestina will never miss me.

Nando greets me warmly with a big embrace and welcomes me inside his home. He has named his baby Dante, just like the famous Italian writer who wrote about heaven and hell. Dante was born May 14, 1913, just days after Emilio Bacchiocchi's funeral.

Oh, it does my heart good to see Nando as a young father, with joy on his face as he takes the little baby from Rosa's arms and shows him to me. I peel back the blanket to see his face.

"He has your eyes, my friend, and look, he has the little dimples in his cheeks, like yours."

"If he's lucky, he will take after his pretty mother and not look like me," Nando says softly, handing him back to his mother.

Nando pours two small glasses of wine and says, "Come, Stefano, we will sit outside and take in the fresh air."

Sitting on the steps, we click our little glasses and said, "*Salute!*" But something about Nando seems distant and sad.

"I hear you don't have the baby baptized, Nando. You don't worry he'll go to hell?"

"I didn't get married in the Church, and I won't let the Church touch my baby. The Church does nothing to help the poor or the working man, just takes his money when he goes to church on Sunday. People with nothing, no roof over their heads, put every penny they have in the collection box, like fools, so Father Petrarca and the others can be rich, live like kings. I will piss on my baby's head before I let a priest baptize my baby."

"Nando! You mustn't talk like that."

"No? You know what that Father Petrarca did? He went to the town, told them to stop our labor meetings at the Driving Park Hall. He denounces us, the anarchists and socialists, our God-given right to strike and to have free speech. He says the town must ban our meetings. He is a traitor to all Italians."

Nando goes silent for a while, looking down at his glass of wine and not at me, swirling the wine in the glass. I think, maybe, he is disappointed in me. Maybe he does not believe I am capable of understanding his grievances against the world. And it's true, there is much I don't understand. I don't know why he is so intense, so sure of his beliefs, so unwavering. So unforgiving.

"Nando, my friend, I worry about you. Every day I look in the papers, looking for news about you. And hoping I don't find any. I don't want you to end up like Emilio…"

"You won't find me in the daily news. I don't make big speeches like my friend Arturo. I'm no good at speaking to crowds. I work in the background, where I can do the most good. I'm a quiet man, Stefano. No one will bother me."

"Your actions are not so quiet, Nando. Where will it end?"

"When the wages we get for working like animals are enough to put food on the table. When the bosses don't stand over us with their stopwatches, arrogant, superior, telling us when to eat, when to piss…"

"But Nando, you have a baby now, and a young wife. You need to think about them. I beg you, please, don't leave them without a husband and father. These are dangerous times."

"I do think about my family. All the time. I think about the future life my son will have in this country. And the life your children will have, too, Stefano. I think about them. You know the strikes they had in Lawrence? They paid the police to beat children with clubs. Children! I think about them, Stefano."

"But you have a skilled job, good pay. You have a good life. Why do you risk losing all that?"

He stops for a moment, quietly fingering the rim of his glass.

"I love all people who work, who try to make a better life, put food on the table. The things they suffer, every day, just because they want to work… Why do they have to suffer? I can't sit still and do nothing."

May, June, and July skitter by like frightened animals, waiting for the next cruel blow to strike. But one by one, the men are returning to work. The women are no longer striking, no longer banging pots and pans and waving their umbrellas. The noise makers and agitators have been silenced.

And after all that pain and effort, no one is earning a penny more than they did before. No one's workday is any shorter. The mighty Draper Company, it seems, has won.

Celestina told me this would happen. She said nothing would change. I didn't believe her.

In the summer of 1913, I see lots of smiling faces in the newspaper. It's a big two-page spread. Happy news about Draper and its summer field days and picnics—but they don't mention one thing. Only the English-speaking workers are invited. Not the immigrants.

The newspapers carry large photos of the big events. Elegant women with long white dresses, lace parasols, and gigantic summer hats standing on the sidelines as spectators, clapping with their little, white-gloved hands. Men in white cotton shorts and white shirts, running races, throwing javelins, and playing ball games.

Anyone can see there is no one like us in this happy gathering. Immigrant women don't have white dresses or white hats with silk flowers. And immigrant men don't have white shorts. We wear dark colors that don't show the dirt and sweat of our labors.

It's as if nothing happened earlier this year. Despite the suffering and grief of my neighbors and friends, the terrible strikes of 1913 will soon be all but forgotten.

But not for Nando. He does not forget, and he does not give up. He continues to write articles for *Il Sovversivo*, continues putting on plays with his wife Rosa, and supports all the local activities of the Wobblies. He goes to their meetings as regularly as other people go to church, but with more faith in his cause than most churchgoers I know, and he helps raise money for strikes in other parts of the country. He talks about a big strike at the iron mines in Minnesota.

I have to ask him, "Why do you care about the workers in Minnesota, so many miles away?"

"Do you know what they do to the Italian immigrants? It's slave labor. We are no better off than the slaves who dragged the great stones to build the pyramids. The bosses, they take advantage of us, because the Italian workers don't speak English.

"In Minnesota, the bosses pay you by how much iron you mine. Piece work. But the places that are hard to mine, the most dangerous, they give those to the immigrants. The immigrants work harder than anybody, but the mine has less ore, so the workers produce less iron, and they make the lowest wages of all."

I didn't understand the outrage my friend could feel for people he doesn't know, halfway across the country. But he never stops his work with the Wobblies in our town.

The bigshots in the town of Milford are afraid of more strikes, more trouble, so they do something no one has ever done before. They decide to ban all open-air meetings starting in December.

The Wobblies ignore the order and organize a local meeting at the Driving Park Hall on Cedar Street, all to support those Minnesota iron workers. Nando, for the first time, gets up the nerve to speak publicly, along with two of his friends.

His timing is terrible. Police arrive on the scene. Nando and his friends are arrested and spend three months in jail. It was Nando's first time in jail, and I am afraid it will not be his last.

Lizzie, 1914

I've never had a single good day in my life. Not one. All I have ever done is work.

My name is Lizzie. Or at least, that's what my teachers try and tell me. I don't know why my real name is so hard for my Irish teachers to say. My mamma calls me Elisabetta—that's my name. But ever since I started at the Plains School, I have been called Lizzie.

My little brother, Girolamo, they call him Jerry. That's not the same name, is it? Some people think Jerry is short for Gerald, or Jeremiah, and they write down his name any way they want. Do they ever think to ask him what his name is? No, never.

My big brother Bartolomeo—people call him Albert. Who knows why. It's not even close. My sister Cesarina—it's the female name for "Caesar," in Italian, a proud name, my father's way of honoring his Uncle Cesare. But they couldn't even get the spelling right on her birth certificate. They wrote "Caesarina." No one seems to understand how to say the soft "c" in Italian. It sounds like the "ch" in "cheese." Just to make it easier, my mother lets people call her "Chezz." Sometimes she writes it down as C-H-E-S-A-R-I-N-A.

But that's not her name. It's not her name.

And my papà, Stefano, some people actually call him Steve. Steve? That's a Yankee name! Even my mamma's name has never been said correctly, with that Italian soft "c." Instead it is sometimes Celeste, Celestina, always sounding like a name that starts with an "s." And now—the name that will probably stick—they call her Celia.

Are these Yanks and Irishmen deliberately trying to confuse us, so we don't even know who we are anymore? I wonder sometimes.

Even as a little schoolgirl, I work to bring home money to help the family. My mother shows me how to make May baskets in the spring, pretty hand-woven straw baskets full of fresh flowers with pink bows on top. The teachers let me take them to school and go from classroom to classroom to sell my spring baskets. In the winter, I bring little Christmas wreaths made from pinecones and walnuts still in their shells. I carry them to school on my arms like big bangle bracelets. Sometimes I bring bags of anisette cookies to sell.

I am now used to bringing home pockets full of coins and putting them in my mother's hands.

———————

For as long as I've been able to walk, I've helped my mamma and papà support the family. I have a gift for using my hands. I can watch anyone do something just once—make a tatted lace glove, plant a seedling, or roll out paper-thin pasta for cappelletti—and I know instantly how to do it myself. I am not such a good student, and my English was never very good, but I can do anything with my hands.

I watch my father put the tall stakes in the ground, mostly skinny, young birch branches, and he ties the tomato plants to the stakes with strips of cotton rag. If I live to be one hundred, God willing, I'll still be putting stakes in the ground the same way my father did, growing tall tomato plants, heavy with plum tomatoes, sweet cherry tomatoes, or those nice big beefsteak tomatoes. And I'll be planting flowers and zucchini and anything else I can think of, as long as there is God's good earth beneath my feet.

My reward for my labors is food. Always food. When I'm in a bad mood, my mamma gives me food. When I work hard, I get more food. No wonder the boys tease me for being such a big girl. I love to eat. It's the only pleasure I have.

I remember taking a break from gardening one Saturday. I walked into the house all hot and sweaty, big half-moons of sweat under my arms, and saw on the kitchen table a fruit like nothing I had never seen before. Long instead of round and bright yellow—never saw any fruit that color before. It was the first time I ever saw bananas.

My father had brought home a massive bunch of bananas from Boston. He always liked to go to Haymarket Square on Saturday mornings, mingle among the Italian pushcart vendors, just to hear the sound of Italian being spoken, and he'd try to get a bargain on something he couldn't grow himself. These bananas were at the point of perfect yellow ripeness—I had never tasted anything like them. Like a creamy pudding inside. I couldn't stop eating them.

Mamma was ready to fly into a rage when she saw all the banana peels I had tossed aside, but my papà said, "Eat, eat! A day will come when we have no food. Eat while you can!" I get the feeling he knows something about going hungry, but he doesn't ever like to talk about it.

———————

My father has a horse-drawn cart that he uses for his errands and for farm work. That horse works as hard as I do, pulls the plow through the soil the way they used to do in the Old Country, or so my father tells me. I will never forget that horse because we have something in common.

We both hate snakes.

One day, I am helping my father in the spring gardens. I see a snake, all slimy and slithering through the tall grass. It's probably just a harmless garter snake, but it doesn't matter. I just don't like them. I scream, "*Bestia! Bestia!*" To me, it's a monster.

The snake slinks past the horse, which has the same reaction I do. Terror. It snorts loudly and rears up on its hind legs. Then he panics and runs off, dragging the plow behind him as he escapes down Hayward Street, making a horrible noise as the plow's metal blades scrape against the road. It takes the whole neighborhood to help my papà catch the horse and calm him down enough to bring him home. From that day on, I have to beat a stick in the grass to make sure there are no snakes before my father hitches the plow to the horse.

It doesn't seem fair. The horse is allowed to be afraid of snakes. Not me.

———————

Our Good Name

It isn't enough that I always help my mother with the cooking. That I clean the floors on my hands and knees. That I scrub the babies' dirty diapers against a washboard. That I tag along with my mother to Holliston when she walks five miles to work the cranberry bogs, because paying a nickel for the bus is too much when she only makes fifteen cents a day picking cranberries. That I watch the babies, including little Girolamo and baby Cesarina still swaddled to a board, while my mother drags long burlap bags and fills them with ripe cranberries.

No, that isn't enough. My father wants me to go work at the Milford Shoe Company.

I quit school after fourth grade. The law says that's as far as we have to go. So now I can get a full-time job at the factory and give a helping hand to my family every day.

I am nine years old.

My first day of work, nobody asks me my age. A woman shows me how to thread the sewing machine and change the bobbin. Then she shows me two pieces of leather and how they fit together to become part of a man's shoe. All I have to do is stitch the pieces together and then throw the connected pieces into a drawer at my station.

I think, *this is easy!* Zip, zip, zip, one after another, I guide the leather pieces under the sewing needle and throw my finished pieces into the open drawer. It's fun, a kind of game to see how many I can do before the whistle sounds at the end of the day.

At the end of my first day, the foreman comes to my station and counts the finished pieces in my drawer. Then he looks at the finished work of an older woman sitting next to me. I have stitched three times as many pieces as she has. He fires her on the spot.

I feel bad for her, losing her job like that. That's when I begin to understand my mistake. I am so stupid. I should have slowed down a little. Now they expect that many pieces from me every day, not just my first day. I have to work extra hard to keep up with my own foolish example. I am just a child. What do I know?

When I get home at night I am tired, but my work isn't done. I am just a girl, but I am the oldest girl, and that means I will always be taking care of the younger children. My mother has been making babies every two or three years, and now she's expecting her fifth. And she's only twenty-eight! Who knows when she'll be done? I'll have to help feed and bathe every last one of them, and sew pretty clothes for them when they outgrow their diapers.

Between working at the shoe shop, helping my father with the gardens, and taking care of my sisters and brothers, I don't know if I'll ever have a life of my own. Whenever a grownup asks me what I want to be when I grow up, I think, *I am already grown up.* How much more grown up can I be?

Stefano, 1917

As 1917 rolls in, Nando will soon have bigger worries. A Great War has been brewing in Europe. Finally, in April, I read the headline I had long feared: America will now join in this war. After losing many merchant ships at sea, the U.S. decides to declare war on Germany.

In May, we learn our adopted country will start drafting young men. I am not too worried for myself. I am too old to be a soldier, and besides, only citizens must register. Celestina and I are still citizens of Italy after all these years, like most of our neighbors. Maybe there is a part of us that thinks we will all return to Italy one day.

But some of the local Italian boys are enlisting just the same, to prove their loyalty to the United States of America, even though they don't have to.

These are the years of hard feelings toward Italians. It is hard for me to understand. Sometimes I ask my son Bartolomeo to explain the strange words I read in the papers. Bartó is fourteen now, smart boy. He tells me President Wilson calls us hyphenated Americans. He says Teddy Roosevelt thought so, too. What does that mean? My son explains we are called Italian-Americans, with a hyphen in the middle, which is not so good as being just plain Americans.

Bartó reads to me what President Wilson says: "Any man who carries a hyphen about with him carries a dagger that he is ready to plunge into the vitals of this Republic." What hyphen? I don't know about any hyphen. I never asked for a hyphen. And the ones who put the hyphen on us now say we use those hyphens like daggers?

The newspapers have not-so-nice cartoons that paint Italians as animals, rats, snakes, anarchists, and criminals. As if all of us are traitors to our country. They talk about the Reds, always the Reds. They are afraid we will revolt like the Russians did, as if labor unions fighting for better working conditions are no different from the Red Terror in Russia.

I want to see Nando to ask what he will do about the draft. I want to know how he feels about this war of many countries.

"Maybe you should enlist," I tell Nando. "You are a young man. You can do a service for your country and bring honor to your family. It will help lift your reputation."

Nando turns to me with a look I have never seen before. His eyes are dark and cold.

"This is not a good war, Stefano. This is the war of the Rockefellers, the rich people, the high-class people—they make this war. This is not like the fight for a free country, the George Washington war all those years ago. No. The wars today are all for big businesses, for making money. And what right do we have to go to other countries and kill poor, innocent people? It is wrong to kill, Stefano. War is wrong!"

"You may not have a choice, my friend. I hear they are drafting more young men like you, whether you want to go or not."

"You think this is the only war that is going on, Stefano? You don't know about the bigger war? The war is against us—the poor, the immigrants, the ones who do all the work. The war is against us. They want to say we are criminals and bandits. Bomb throwers. Filthy animals. That's what they think we are.

"It supposed to be free country. Free speech, free thinking. But a man is not allowed to read books and newspapers about the working man and his struggle. My poor Rosina, she so scared, she burning my newspapers and books. Men like me go to jail, just because of how we think and what we read. And you think the war is against Germany? No, Stefano, the war is against *us*."

"But how are you going to fight such a war, Nando?"

"I read *Cronaca Sovversivo*. They tell us what to do. The editor takes a stand against war, all war. There are many men, Italian men, who think like me. We don't believe in war. We will do what *Cronaca* tells us we must do. We will go to Mexico."

"Mexico? Why Mexico?"

"They tell us only Mexico is safe. Mexico stays neutral—they don't go to war. I will go with many other men like me."

"But Rosina? The baby? Your little Dante?"

"They will wait for me."

———————

Nando is loyal to his cause, as I would soon find. Leaving his young family behind, he joins about sixty other men from the United States, all looking for peace and asylum in northern Mexico. I hear he changed his name to Nicola Moscatelli to confuse the authorities; Moscatelli was his mother's maiden name, and Nicola was the name of a favorite brother of his who had died.

And his beloved *Cronaca Sovversiva*, whose editors urged all their readers to refuse the draft as a matter of principle? That newspaper was banned and shut down.

"You see, Stefano? What do I tell you?" I can hear his voice in my head, telling me this. "There is no free speech, no free press, not in your United States of America. They are free press for the Yankee newspapers that prop up the rich, the powerful. Not for *Cronaca,* the voice of men like me. No free press for us."

But after only four months in Mexico, he misses his pretty wife and his baby boy too much—I could have predicted this—and he returns to join them. Celestina has been writing letters to Nando's wife Rosa. She tells me Rosa has been staying in Cambridge, Massachusetts, in a safe house, offered to them by a friend who is sympathetic to Nando's cause. Now Nando will join them. He is keeping his new name Nicola, though.

He is now known as Nicola Sacco.

I can never get used to that name. For me, he is always my friend Ferdinando, or simply Nando. And knowing what I know now, I wish he had stayed in Mexico.

Celestina, 1920

The year began with a feeling of worry. An unspoken horror that filled every corner of my heart.

I have a little bit of the gypsy fortuneteller in me. I can see the future sometimes. I can read the omens and signs, like that single black crow I saw in my cherry tree on the day of Emilio's funeral. That crow visits me all the time now, reminding me there are more dark days to come. I know this year will not end well. And the troubles, like most troubles, will come in a group of three.

My family will be visited by three dark angels this year.

I should be feeling a sense of peace. The Great War is over. My family is growing. We have five healthy children. We never go without food on our table. We have chickens, pigs, and a goat. We have sausages drying in the attic, a cellar full of root vegetables, canned goods that I put up myself, and my Stefano's sweet homemade wine.

My two growing sons are strong and help work the land, and they do piecework in the factories, too. Bartolomeo, whose Yankee name is Albert, is now sixteen, tall and lean, and popular with the pretty girls. Girolamo, known to others as Jerry, is twelve and has his brother's dark wavy hair and strong Roman nose, curved like an eagle's beak. He is almost as tall as his brother. To see the two boys together, from a little distance, you might think they are twins. My good daughter Elisabetta, the one they call Lizzie, is fourteen, almost a woman, strong and stout. She has been working in the shoe factory for five years already, all the while helping me with my gardens and being a second mother to her two younger sisters—Cesarina, who is eight, and little Irena, who is five.

We have everything our family could ask for. Good health, a house of our own, and land that is rich and good to us. Both my parents still live across the street from my house. My little sister Mary and her husband live with them, along with their little boy John. They named him John after my poor brother Giovanni, who died in the bicycle accident. My cousin, Giovanni Marenghi from Pereto, moved into their house when there was no more room for him in my house. I am surrounded by a growing family, all within sight or just a short walk from my front door.

As we enter the new year, we hear that my niece Rosina has been feeling poorly. That's nothing new. She's been sickly for years. Two years ago we worried she had the Spanish influenza, the famous grip. Milford lost almost one hundred people to the grip in 1918—more than the number of our boys who died in the Great War.

I always thought the deaths from the grip were many more than what they say in the newspapers. I heard someone say the newspapers tried to keep the death count small so we don't look like a weak country to our enemies. You had to wonder why so many people, including young people, were suddenly dying of "pneumonia." That's not what I think was really killing them.

I remember there was a Mr. Higgiston from the Board of Health. We saw him go from door to door on Hayward Street, Mount Pleasant Street, East Main—all the streets around my house. Everyone knew who he was. He might as well have been wearing a dark hooded cape and carrying a scythe of death because his job was to see death wherever he went. Old women thought he was cursed, bringing death to their streets and not just reporting it. He wrote down what he saw and sent it to the *Milford Daily News*.

He told the newspaper that he saw a house in my neighborhood where a little girl lay dead. He didn't say her name, but I think I know. All the neighbors had come to the girl's wake to pay their respects. I went there, too, along with many of my neighbors, all ages, including the little children who went to school with the girl. Higgiston wrote a letter to the editor, in his fancy way of talking, to say, "He asks the

News to make plain that such gatherings in infected homes are simply suicide for many little ones."

I always look for the Italian names among the dead. The newspaper never likes to mention Italians in their pages, as if we don't exist. Maybe they think if they don't write about us, we'll disappear and go away. If you have a nice Yankee name, it's different. You can go on a summer vacation, and they'll write a big story about it. If you're Italian, you can be born, get married, or die, and the news won't even mention it.

But nothing escapes the eyes of Italian women who speak the daily news from porch to porch. We hear names like Iadarola, Ruggiero, Cenedella, Grillo. All dying from the grip. These names don't appear in the newspapers.

Antonio De Pasquale, who runs one of the funeral homes, said there were so many dead bodies brought to his door, he couldn't handle them all. They say he asked boys from the highway department to build a mass grave at the St. Mary's Cemetery and lay all the bodies in there in long trenches. No one could ever say if it's true or where this big grave might be hiding.

The grip raged for two years, rising and falling, but I think it never really went away. Even now, in 1920, I am still afraid the grip will find its way to my family. We are poor people, workers in field and factory who have to leave the house every day. We can't afford to stay home in bed and drink cups of hot chocolate all day, like our superior townspeople in the big houses uptown, who criticize us for not staying home. The influenza was bound to find us, and Rosina was the most likely to catch it—always complaining of headaches, always a weariness in her bones.

In January, when the snow buries the ground and the cold wraps its strong arms around the houses, I hear Rosina is having trouble getting out of bed. Albina has sent her twelve-year-old daughter Desolina to look after Rosina's children so that Rosina can get some rest. Rosina has three little ones—Alessandro, Maria Rosa, and Pietro, all under the age of six.

I go to see Rosina, but she doesn't want me to see her lying in bed. She is stubborn. She wants to get up to make me some tea in her kitchen. But she can't even walk a few steps without struggling for breath. She is sucking the air hard like she is breathing through a blocked hose. I make her go back to her bed. I help her lift her feet back under the covers, and I notice her ankles are swollen, like when she was pregnant.

"Look at your ankles, Rosina. Are you expecting?"

"I don't know. I feel the same kind of tired. Like the life has been drained out of me."

At first, I tell her husband not to worry too much. Rosina always seemed to tire easily. And maybe it's good news, I say. Maybe she is pregnant again. But Giuseppe knows his wife better than I do. He calls Doctor Goslin to come to their house. The doctor puts a stethoscope to Rosina's chest and says he hears palpitations.

Dr. Goslin visits Rosina every single day for the next nine days. On the tenth day, he signs her death certificate. She is just twenty-seven years old.

The doctor says it was her heart and a case of rheumatism in her bones. He does not say it was the Spanish influenza, but I think it was. I will never change my mind. I think the grip weakened her poor heart and crept into her bones. I don't think anyone wants to admit how many of us died from the grip because no one cares how many Italians die. But I know it was many, many more than the numbers they print in the newspapers.

The news of her death turns me inside out. I can't make sense of all the things I feel. I am lost, confused, angry, sad. I am too shaken to be of much good to anyone. I should be cooking a big pot of soup and bringing it to Giuseppe and the children, but I can't move. I can't do anything.

Rosina was like a daughter to me, or a younger sister, living under my roof as one of my own. I want to picture her as she once was, the pretty girl bringing a tray of wine glasses and cookies out to the grape arbor for Stefano. The girl who blushed easily and lowered her soft brown eyes when she spoke. I miss her coming home from work and sitting down at the table with me, telling me all about her day.

My Stefano takes it even harder. He feels he was responsible for watching over his brother's little girl. He believes he has failed his brother. He is crying bitterly when he tells me this.

"I remember how I worried for her. I told her Giuseppe was too old. He would make her a widow before her time. She would have been lucky to live so long!"

The image of Rosina as a widow brings fresh grief to his eyes.

"I just wanted Rosina to find a man who would take care of her, make her happy," Stefano says. "I thought she had found such a man. She would be safe now. Set for life."

"We all thought so, Stefano."

"My poor brother! I know how much Pietro will suffer, knowing he sent his daughter far away for a better life, only for her to die so young in her New Country."

We can't spend too much time mourning when Giuseppe and his children need our help. I agree to write letters to the family in Italy to let them know. I have to find the words to tell Pietro and Amalia that the daughter they have not seen in twelve years is lost to them. The words I write seem foolish and useless. Our hearts are broken, I say. I give dates, times, the bare facts.

Stefano signs his name next to mine, his handwriting shaky and uneven like that of an old man. It will be weeks before Pietro gets the letter, but I already know the ache he will feel. I know because Rosina was like my own flesh and blood.

Albina writes the letters to her sisters and brothers. She lives in Hopedale now with Domenico and their five children. She writes first to Tranquilla, who lives in Bridgewater, Massachusetts, with her husband Eugenio Resmini. Albina has two more sisters and two brothers still in Italy.

Giuseppe asks Stefano to be one of the pall bearers. Rosina is so small and light, they hardly need six men to carry her, but there will be six. In addition to Stefano and Giuseppe, my son Bartolomeo, Tranquilla's husband Eugenio, Albina's husband Domenico, and Stefano's cousin Giovanni are pall bearers. As they carry her to her funeral Mass at Sacred Heart, with so many of our neighbors from the Plains filling the church, a sea of black shawls and black coats, I could feel the angel of death sitting beside me. It was reminding me. There are two more angels to come.

It is cold as a mother-in-law's hands on the day of her funeral, with fifteen inches of snow on the frozen ground. Poor Rosina will have to be placed in the St. Mary's Cemetery vault and wait until the spring thaw before her grave can be dug.

Celestina, 1920

As winter comes to an end, I often think of little Rosina, waiting patiently in her coffin for the ground to thaw and open up a space for her final resting place. I wish our friends Nando and Rosa were still in Milford so I could talk to Rosa about my niece. He never said so, but I think Nando was sweet on her. But he frightened her away with all his big ideas about labor unions and politics. I know Stefano misses his friend Nando, too, and their conversations under the grape arbor. Nando would be a comfort to him. Sometimes my father comes over and sits with Stefano, but it's not the same. Stefano never had a friend like Nando.

It is April, and the maple trees are sprouting fresh yellow-green leaves, the forsythia is flashing bright yellow, and the purple grape hyacinths are popping up in the flower beds. Spring always makes me think of better times to come. Our beloved Bing cherry tree has already lost most of its white blossoms in the April rains. The reddish-black fruit will soon follow. It is something I can always be sure about, the perfect sweet fruit of my cherry tree, as reliable as the four seasons. I only wish Rosina could be here to see it.

But before the cherries can grow heavy and ripen, the second dark news of the year arrives, killing my hopes of the season and prolonging my grief over Rosina with a renewal of sorrow. It is just as I had predicted. There would be not one but three dark angels visiting us this year. This time, the news comes in a letter sealed in a light-brown envelope with a postmark from Italy, a red and white stamp with the image of Vittorio Emanuele III.

It is addressed to Stefano. He asks our son Bartolomeo to read it aloud. A letter from Italy is a big occasion, so all our children gather around so they can hear what is in the letter, too.

As Bartolomeo's eyes scan the length of the letter, I watch his bright expression darken. He looks up and says, "I don't want to read this to you."

"Read it, read it!" I say.

My son swallows hard and tries to gather his strength. "It's from Amalia. I don't read Italian so good. Mamma, please, you read it."

He hands the letter to me; I look sideways at him. He never had trouble reading Italian before. But I take the letter, stand up, and begin to read.

> *Dear Stefano,*
>
> *By the time you get this letter, my loving husband Pietro, your dear brother, will be dead and buried in the ground.*

I stop for a moment and look at Stefano. This news is a complete shock. We knew nothing about Pietro being ill. We had no warning of this. Stefano shows no immediate reaction, but I wonder if he understands what he has just heard. I continue reading:

> *I am so sorry, my dear Stefano. I think the loss of our dear Rosina may have hurried my husband a little faster to his grave.*
> *Pietro was stubborn. His heart was weak, but he never told us. He was too proud. He defied death to the end. By the time he could conceal his pain no longer, the doctor told us it would be hours, not days. But he did not accept that. He lived another week, refusing to let go of this life. I was at his side, and he was still gripping my hand after his last breath had left him.*
> *I wanted to let you know it was Pietro's wish not to tell you he was dying. Our Uggero was ready to run to the post office, to send you the news by telegram. But Pietro knew it would be a hardship for you to travel to Italy, so soon after you paid for our Rosina's funeral, and after all the suffering you endured. Even if you had*

the money, coming to us by boat would take too long, and you would never have been here in time.

Please do not be angry at us for following his wishes. He wanted us to wait until he was buried to send you this letter. He thought it would make you suffer too much to tell you sooner. For you to know your brother was dying and to have no way to get to him before he died—that was an ache he wanted to spare you.

We laid him in his coffin with his favorite tobacco and pipe, a sack of dried plums from our yellow plum tree, his walking stick, and a photo of your mother. Do your children understand our custom? How we bury people with their favorite belongings so their spirits won't come back to look for them? I don't know if you buried our Rosina that way.

Pietro was the rock that held our family together, and he would want us to be strong. Grazie a Dio, *we have our children to help us through this sorrow.*

I have sent letters to my girls, Tranquilla and Albina. I cannot embrace them with my own arms. I ask you and Celestina to hold them close for me.

My love to you, to Celestina, and to all your children.

When I look up from the letter, Stefano has slumped forward in his chair and tumbles suddenly to the floor. He seems to have fainted! I ask my boys to help me carry him to the couch in the front parlor. I lift his feet to the couch and place a pillow under them.

I open his shirt collar so he can breathe better, all the while calling his name. "Stefano, Stefano! Wake up, Stefano!"

Lizzie brings a wet cloth, and I help her lay it over her Stefano's forehead. The cloth is cold, and it seems to spark a reaction. Stefano seems to be coming around, moaning softly. I slap my husband's face gently and say, "Wake up! Wake up!"

"What? Where am I?" he asks.

"You fainted, Stefano. Are you alright? Can you hear me?"

"What? No, I was just… the letter. It was from my brother, no?" He looks wobbly and tries to sit up.

"The letter. I don't think I heard the whole thing. It is from Pietro. He is coming to see me. He is finally coming to see my big American house! Did he say he is coming by boat? That's what he said. I remember now. He said it is expensive and takes too long, but he is coming. He is coming here at last."

"Lizzie, run for the doctor."

"Isn't my brother coming to see me? He is bringing his favorite things. His pipe. His dried plums. He wants to see my house. He has never seen my house. I have to make everything ready." Stefano tries to stand up, but he is too unsteady.

"Albert, Jerry, help me hold him down. We have to keep him here till the doctor comes."

"I have to get up. So much to do. But something is holding me down. Who are these people holding me down? Let me go!"

Lizzie has brought a glass of red wine. I press it to my husband's lips.

"Here, drink, drink, *amore mio.* It will calm you. Drink, and everything will be better in the morning."

The wine trickles into Stefano's mouth and throat. He doesn't swallow it. It simply pours into his mouth and down his throat. I hope it radiates warmth and softens his confusion and pain.

Celestina, 1920

It started with a robbery in Braintree, Massachusetts.

On May 26, 1920, the *Milford Daily News* gives the story front-page space. At first, I don't know why this is such big news in Milford. Our town is some forty miles away from Braintree. The article says that four men are arrested for stealing $16,000 in payroll money from a Braintree factory. It seems like a big cops-and-robbers story, just like something in the movies. Two men are shot and killed. The robbers escape in a speeding black car. Then two men are captured on a trolley car and arrested for the crime. One of the men is identified as Mike Saco of South Stoughton. Another is Bert Vanzetti of Plymouth.

I don't know anyone named Mike Saco. But the most reliable news criers—the Italian women on our street—quickly share the word that "Mike Saco" is none other than my husband's old friend Ferdinando Sacco.

The news seems unbelievable to Stefano.

"I don't care what your friends say. This not my friend Ferdinando, the one who didn't have the heart to kill a chicken. It is not in his heart to do such a thing."

"This is the same man, Stefano. The papers say he met Vanzetti in Mexico. You know Nando went to Mexico. The story must be true."

"Lots of men go to Mexico. This is not my friend Nando."

My Stefano is stubborn. But I know. The newspapers say the men are anarchists, dangerous men. They think they planned to steal the money for their terrorist cause. They say Vanzetti is a fish monger and Sacco is a shoemaker. That sounds like Ferdinando to me.

The newspaper stories say other things, too. They remind everyone about the Palmer Raids, the Red Scare, the bombings in public places that are always blamed on Italians. I don't know why every story about one Italian has to be linked either directly or by sly suggestion with bombings in different places by completely different people. Do they think all Italians are connected to each other by invisible threads, as if we are all one terrible interconnected animal? Some poisonous spreading virus? What do all those violent events in other parts of the world have to do with two poor Italian immigrants in the little state of Massachusetts?

"There are lots of Saccos," Stefano insists. "There's even another Nicola Sacco right in this town. They must have the wrong one. My friend is a gentle, honorable man. He holds out his arm to old women walking to church. He would not shoot a man."

It is not until the newspapers publish photographs of the two men that Stefano begins to understand his friend is in very serious trouble. He still thinks they have the wrong man. He is sure the charges will be dismissed quickly, a case of mistaken identity.

But I know differently. The charges will stick. I just know it.

The third and final angel I had predicted has come to call and darken my door. It is the heaviest and cruelest angel of all, striking my Stefano hard while he is still burdened with his brother's and niece's passing.

One night, we are sitting down for our dinner, surrounded by our five children. Once again, Stefano starts going on and on about mistaken identity, how they have the wrong man in jail. I am so tired of hearing this, I can't stay quiet any longer.

"Stefano, wake up! It was clear all along! We always knew it would end this way. He was always asking for trouble!"

At this, Stefano stands up and pounds the table with his fist. "*Bugiarda!* I will cut the tongue out of your mouth if you ever speak of my friend that way again!"

The table suddenly goes from lively chattering to dead silence. I have never seen such rage from my gentle husband's mouth. My children and I sit frozen in fear, not touching our food or moving in any way, until Stefano finishes his meal and rises to leave the room.

In the days that follow, Stefano and I barely speak. I see him read the papers every day with great attention, looking for proof that, somehow, they have the wrong man in jail. He expects every day to see the headline, "A Case of Mistaken Identity." Sometimes I try and look over his shoulder to see what he is reading, but I know. And it's not the news he is looking for.

The trial begins in June. Some of the Foggianos from the Plains district go to the trial in Dedham every day. Whenever Stefano encounters any of them passing by our house, he stops and asks them if they know what is happening.

I hear one of them tell Stefano about the first day of the trial. As the crowd was moving toward the courthouse, someone pointed up to the roof, and then everyone looked up at once. There were armed guards dressed in black, standing in a row on the edge of the roof, like menacing black crows with rifles pointing down at the crowd. I think they would not have hesitated for one minute to rain bullets down on every Italian they saw. I am glad Stefano decided not to go.

Sometimes I ask one of the Foggiano neighbors myself what happened in court that day, what they saw and heard. They say it is total confusion. An Italian interpreter is supposed to be telling Sacco and Vanzetti what is happening in Italian and also interpret their statements into English for the court. But the interpreter they picked doesn't understand that Sacco speaks a Foggiano dialect, something only understood by other Foggianos. Vanzetti comes from northern Italy, where they speak an entirely different dialect. Vanzetti speaks English a little better than Sacco, and is a little more educated, but still the crowd is always yelling corrections to the interpreters' statements. The judge is always banging his big wooden hammer, demanding "Quiet in the court!"

I remember Emilio Bacchiocchi and the murderer who went unpunished. His family had no justice. Now I fear it will not go well for Sacco and Vanzetti. An Italian immigrant's life is not worth much in the eyes of a Yankee judge, in this case, a man named Webster Thayer. He makes no secret of his hatred for Italians and for immigrants.

These men are not on trial for murder. They are on trial for being born Italian.

Ninety-nine witnesses for the accused, mostly Italian, testify to their innocence. They say both Sacco and Vanzetti were in other places, far from the scene of the crime. Sacco was at the Italian Consulate in Boston, applying for a passport so he can visit his sick father in Italy. He was there with his wife Rosa and son Dante, and they even had a family passport photo taken at the consulate. Witnesses saw them at the photographer's studio, and others saw them later having lunch in a little restaurant in Boston. Vanzetti was doing his daily work as a fishmonger, with dozens of Italian housewives swearing they bought fish from him the day of the murders, some 25 miles from the scene of the crime.

But all these witnesses are Italian immigrants themselves. So their testimony is dismissed as if it means nothing. An Irish boy who delivered newspapers that day says he saw two men who looked like the Italians on trial, even though they were inside a speeding getaway car.

The boy's words are given greater weight than all the testimonies from Italians.

Ferdinando, 1920

I wish the citizens of this great country could understand that I am a man of intelligence. I have read books, many books, on literature, art, history, and astronomy. I have a passion for philosophy and political discourse. I named my son after the magnificent Dante Alighieri, the greatest writer the world has ever known. Is that the mark of an un-educated man?

But when I open my mouth, my broken English does not match my thoughts. My tongue betrays me, making people think I am not their equal. My fondest wish is that my sons and grandsons will be educat-ed at one of the world's finest institutes of learning, like Harvard or Yale, or maybe one of the ancient universities of Europe. I want them to have beautiful homes filled with shelves and shelves of books. I hope my boy Dante will grow to be as eloquent as the one who wrote *La Divina Commedia*—that is something that I, a poor shoemaker, will never achieve.

For years I have watched my countrymen, good Italians, arrested, im-prisoned, and deported from the United States because we are falsely branded as terrorists. And those who try to lead us toward justice are stopped at every turn. I think about Eugene Debs, one of the greatest thinkers who ever lived. He founded the Industrial Workers of the World, the one they call the Wobblies, so the working class would have a voice. He was a founding member of every socialist movement in this country. He ran for president as the Socialist candidate five times, the last time from jail. They threw him in jail because of what he thinks.

And this happens in America.

I will tell you who the real terrorists are: the ones who hold power, in governments, in big businesses, who round us up and hold us in chains because of our beliefs. They *say* they are protecting this country from the bloody revolution that happened in Russia. What they are really doing is denying the free speech and free thinking that will allow peaceful change and a better life for hard-working men and women. They have money and wear nice clothes, but they are no better that the angry mobs that speak only the language of violence and destruction.

All this is on my mind today as I give my testimony at the Dedham Superior Court. District Attorney Frederick Katzmann will do his best to paint me as an ignorant immigrant and make me trip on my words. I don't trust the interpreter they hired, so I will speak in English as much as I can, and I will draw strength from the many Italian countrymen watching me from their benches and standing in the back of the room. Some of them I recognize from my days in Milford. Some from Cambridge and Stoughton.

I testify on their behalf as well.

These are some of my words as the court reporter took them down. I apologize for my poor broken English.

Q: Did you say yesterday you love a free country?
A: *Yes, sir.*

Q: Did you love this country in May 1917? Did you go to Mexico in May 1917 to avoid being a soldier for this country that you say you love?
A: *Yes.*

Q: And would it be your idea of showing your love for your wife that, when she needed you, you ran away from her?
A: *I did not run away from her.*

Q: Don't you think going away from your country is a vulgar thing to do when your wife and son need you?
A: *I don't believe in war.*

Q: You don't believe in war?

A: *No, sir.*

Q: Do you think it is a cowardly thing to do what you did?

A: *No, sir.*

Q: Do you think it is a brave thing to do what you did?

A: *Yes, sir.*

Judge Webster Thayer: All I ask is this one question, and it will simplify matters very much. Is it your claim that in your collection of subversive literature and the books and papers, that that was done in the interest of the United States? Mr. Katzmann, I will let you inquire further first as to what he meant by the expression.

Q: What did you mean when you said yesterday you loved a free country?

A: *Give me a chance to explain.*

When I was in Italy, a boy, I was a Republican, so I always thinking Republican has more chance to manage education, develop, to build someday his family, to raise the child and education, if you could. But that was my opinion; so when I came to this country, I saw Republican was not what I was thinking before, but there was all the difference because I been working in Italy not so hard as I been working in this country.

I could live free there just as well. Work in the same condition but not so hard, about seven or eight hours a day, better food. Of course, over here is good food because it is bigger country, to any those who got money to spend, not for the working and laboring class, and in Italy is more opportunity to laborer to eat vegetables, more fresh, and then I came in this country.

When I been started work here very hard and been work thirteen years, hard worker, I could not afford much a family the way I did have the idea before. I could not put any money in the bank. I could not push my boy some to go to school and other things. I teach over here men who is with me. The free idea gives any man a chance to profess his own idea, not the supreme idea, not to give any person, not to be like Spain in position, yes, about twenty centuries ago, but to give a chance to print and education, literature, free speech, that I see it was all wrong.

I could see the best men, intelligent, educated. They been arrested and sent to prison and died in prison for years and years without getting them out, and Mr. Debs, one of the great men in his country, he is in prison, still away in prison, because he is a Socialist. He say no to the war, and they call him a spy. He wanted the laboring class to have better conditions and better living, more education, give a push his son if he could have a chance someday, but they put him in prison.

Why? Because the capitalist class, they know they are against that, because the capitalist class, they don't want our child to go to high school or college or Harvard College. There would be no chance, there would not be no—they don't want the working class educationed, they want the working class to be a low all the times, be underfoot, and not to be up with the head. So, sometimes, you see, the Rockefellers, Morgans, they give fifty—I mean they give five hundred thousand dollars to Harvard College, they give a million dollars for another school. Every day say, 'Well, Rockefeller is a great man, the best man in the country.'

I want to ask him, who is going to Harvard College? What benefit the working class they will get by those million dollars they give by Rockefeller? They won't get, the poor class, they won't have no chance to go to Harvard College because men who is getting twenty-one dollars a week or thirty dollars a week, I don't care if he gets eighty dollars a week, if he gets a family of five children, he can't live and send his child and go to Harvard College if he wants to eat everything nature will give him. If he wants to eat like a cow, and that is the best thing, but I want men to live like men.

I like men to get everything that nature will give best, because they belong—we are not the friend of any other place, but we belong to nations. So that is why my idea has been changed. So that is why I love people who labor and work and see better conditions every day develop, makes no more war. We no want fight by the gun, and we don't want to destroy young men. The mother has been suffering for building the young man. Somedays need a little more bread, so when the time the mother get some bread or profit out of that boy, that's when the Rockefellers, Morgans, and some of the peoples, high class, they send him to war.

Why? What is war? The war is not shoots like Abraham Lincoln's and Abe Jefferson, to fight for the free country, for the better education to give chance to any other peoples, not the white people but the black and the others, because they believe and know they are men like the rest, but they are war for the great millionaire. No war for the civilization of men. They are war for business, million dollars come on the side.

What right we have to kill each other?

I been work for the Irish. I have been working with the German fellow, with the French, many other peoples. I love them people just as I could love my wife, and my people for that did receive me. Why should I go kill them men? What he done to me? He never done anything, so I don't believe in no war. I want to destroy all the guns.

That is why I like people who want education and living, building, who is good, just as much as they could. That is all.

Q: And that is why you love the United States of America?
A: *Yes.*

Q: And without the light of knowledge on the subject, you are condemning even Harvard University, are you, as being a place for rich men? Did you intend to condemn Harvard College?
A: *No, sir.*

Q: Were you ready to say none but the rich could go there?
A: *I cannot say yes or no.*

Q: Is it because you can't or because you don't want to?
A: *Because it is a very delicate question.*

Q: And the books which you intended to collect were books relating to anarchy, weren't they?
A: *Not all of them.*

Q: How many of them?

A: *Well, all together, socialists, democratic, any other socialistic information, Syndicalists, Anarchists, any paper.*

Q: Bolshevist?

A: *I do not know what Bolshevist means.*

Q: Soviet?

A: *I do not know what Soviet means.*

Q: Communism?

A: *Yes. And I got some books on astronomy, too.*

Q: You weren't going to destroy them?

A: *I was going to keep them.*

Q: You were going to keep them, and when the time was over, you were going to bring them out again, weren't you?

A: *Yes.*

Q: And you say you don't believe in war?

A: *No, I don't believe in war. What right we have to kill anybody?*

Celestina, 1926

I know what the world is like. I see with clear eyes. Not Stefano. He's always been too tender-hearted. For five years after they convicted his old friend, the one the world now calls Nicola Sacco, he read about the hunger strikes, the appeals, the protests in every country of the world. I know his friend is doomed, not a doubt in my mind, and that we will one day see the news of his electrocution at the hands of pink-faced Yankees with fiery red hatred in their hearts.

Stefano doesn't need to think about that. I try to hide the *Milford Daily News*. I shift it around the house so my children can read it, but my husband can't. He always used to enjoy reading the newspaper, saying it helped him learn English, but I think he already has enough on his mind. It upsets him too much. I have seen him fly into a rage, ranting like an idiot when he reads a headline he doesn't like.

One headline that set him off was about a negro man who was lynched in the South.

He said, "Why do they say a 'negro' was lynched? Why not say a *man* was lynched? And why do they say an 'Italian' was caught for stealing an apple? Isn't he just a man, too? A Chinaman does this, a Negro does that, an Italian does one thing or the other. Why don't they just call them men?

"I think my friend Nando was right. There's a war against us. All of us who don't speak good English, who don't have money, who aren't born here. They think we're not white, like them. That's what they think. Look at me, with my freckles and my white skin that turns red in the sun, and my red hair. They think I'm not white! They want to lynch us Italians, too!"

"What are you babbling about? They lynch the colored people, not Italians."

I respond. "I tell you they'll lynch Italians whatever chance they get. I'll get Bartó to look it up in the library. You'll see!"

I don't know what goes on in that head of his most of the time. Lynching Italians. Ridiculous.

Stefano is in his fifties now, but he looks so much older. Still wearing that silly Alpine hat with the feather, looking like a man who just came off the boat from the Old Country.

How I worry for him, day after day. Since the three dark angels came to visit us, he has edged closer and closer to losing his mind. His drinking has gone from secret hidden swigs in the wine cellar to openly carrying around his bottle, not even bothering with a drinking glass, like some pathetic wino you trip over on the sidewalk. He has no shame anymore.

His bottle is just one of his two escapes. The other is my flesh. In 1920, that horrible year, he began attacking my body every single night with a hunger you cannot imagine, like a man on fire. A man in his fifties, acting like someone half his age. The old fool. So strong was his passion, he impregnated me twice as hard, leaving me with twins. I knew it from the start. I felt their weight and movement long before they were born. My belly stretched out in front of me like a tugboat pulling my exhausted body behind it.

Attilio and Matilda were born in July 1921. But Attilio is thin and weak, as if Matilda had consumed all the nourishment of my womb and left her little brother with nothing. Poor Attilio didn't live more than a day. And my Stefano, after four daughters, had been so hopeful for another son. I was hoping for a sweet little boy, too. We will have to love our Matilda—we call her Tillie—at least twice as much to make up for losing her twin.

But my days of producing daughters is far from over. I am forty years old when I give birth to little Caterina Anna. I hoped this would be the end of my husband's nightly assaults on my body, for that is how I now feel about his advances. They are assaults, clumsy, forceful, and unwelcome. His body is heavy, a deadweight crushing my bones, clutching me without feeling or tenderness, making it hard for me to breathe. And always he is drunk from his homemade wine.

His sour breath smells terrible when he comes to bed, and he doesn't bathe as often as he should. I can't stand to be near him anymore. The man I held close to my body every night for twenty-three years, the only man who had ever touched me, is no longer a welcome presence in my bed. When I was a young woman, I used to like joining my body to his. Now I pray every time he will finish his business quickly and allow me a little sleep.

––––––––––––

Caterina is sucking hard at my breast when my sister Mary comes running across the street one morning and pounds on my side door. It is Wednesday, November 10, 1926. A date I will long remember. Mary still lives at my parents' house, along with her husband Louis Speroni and their two little boys. She is a young woman; her face is flush with November's chill. She hadn't bothered putting on a jacket.

"Celestina, come quick! It's Papà!"

I wrap a heavy knit shawl around my shoulders and drape it over the baby, and then follow her across the street. Mary leads me to the small kitchen in the back, where my poor father is lying on his side on the floor. There is a broken cup and a pool of brown liquid on the floor, and my father appears to be sleeping peacefully despite the loud wailing of his wife. My mother is on her knees, leaning over her husband, sobbing horribly with great gulping sounds. I hand baby Caterina to Mary and help my mother to her feet, coaxing her to sit with me on a sofa in the living room.

"He was drinking coffee at the table with us, normal, *come sempre*," when suddenly he fell off the chair," Mary said. "We tried to wake him, but he was just as you see him now. Not a move, not a breath. Like a bolt of lightning hit him."

"Give me back the baby, Mary, and go run for the doctor. I'll stay here with Mamma."

"But my sons will be home from school soon."

"Then go quickly!" I snap. "Can't you see I have enough on my hands here?"

I adjust baby Caterina on my left hip and go to fetch a glass of water for my mother. I sit with her sobbing against my shoulder until Mary returns with the doctor. Mary leads the doctor to the kitchen, and then the doctor comes back to tell us what we already know.

"I will call for an undertaker," the doctor offered.

"No, that is not necessary," I say. "We will prepare his body here."

"You will not consider…"

"We will take care of it," I say firmly.

I don't know where my voice comes from, sounding like the commander of an army, giving orders instead of crying tears of sadness for my father. I think my mother and sister are happy to have me take charge. They never know what to do without me. I will keep them busy so they don't think about crying so much. Crying can wait.

I tell my sister to go to the house of Antonio DePasquale on Cedar Street. Antonio and his sons are all undertakers. We will need a coffin. The DePasquales will bring us the coffin. And I tell Mary the names of the women we know who will come help us wash the body of my father. We will need several strong women.

I tell my mother we need to go to her bedroom and find my father's best clothes. I help her find my father's suit, the one he wore to his children's weddings, and she lays it out on the bed. With one arm still holding my baby, I pull out drawers looking for clean underwear and a good shirt. All of this is laid out on the bed.

"That's good, Mamma. That's good. Now we go downstairs and wait."

Before long, the women are arriving. I love the way women always know what to do without anyone telling them, all of them rushing into action and doing whatever needs to be done. Like a school of fish, all moving together with the same purpose. The coffee on the floor is being mopped up. A kettle of water is heating on the stove. A wash tub is being filled. Clean towels and bars of soap appear. My sister Mary is kneeling on the floor, holding our father's head on her lap and tenderly washing his face, while others gently remove his shoes and clothes. My father will be washed and dressed before the undertakers arrive.

Without saying a word, I wrap myself and Caterina in my shawl and quietly leave. I walk back to my house, where I hand my baby to Cesarina as if I am delivering a parcel and ignore whatever she is saying to me. I can't hear anything. I climb the stairs with slow, heavy, weary steps and find my way to my bedroom.

Only then do I collapse onto my knees, alone in the center of the floor, and unpour my soul, my delayed grief. My love for my father, so deeply felt yet rarely spoken aloud, is now gushing out of me. I am weeping like a child into my hands.

It's funny how we sometimes don't know things about our own family until we read them in the paper. My father died of heart failure. That's what the paper said. I never even thought to ask the doctor. My father was sixty-seven years old. I hadn't thought about his age, either, until I read it.

To my surprise, he had already purchased a burial plot at St. Mary's Cemetery. How did I not know this? My parents lived across the street and I saw them almost every day. Of all the things we talked about, we never talked about death. It's not until we go see the priest about the funeral mass that he tells us about the cemetery plot. Without telling anyone, not even his wife and children, he planned ahead.

My poor mother never really could think straight after losing her favorite son in that bicycle accident. Maybe my father didn't trust her to take care of financial matters. I think that's why he encouraged Mary and her family to stay in the house for years after they were married. He knew they would help take care of his wife.

Weeks after we bury my father, I am to be surprised again. It seems my father made a will, all signed and sealed at the lawyer's office in downtown Milford. A will! Who could have imagined he was such a modern man?

The day comes when I must sit with my brother Giuseppe, my sister Mary, and our mother in the lawyer's office as he begins to read aloud the document. "I, Luigi Antonio Mario Abretti, being of sound mind and body."

The lawyer stops and looks up at us, with our shabby coats and well-worn shoes. I wonder if he is thinking we are backward immigrants who might not be capable of understanding the legal language.

"Let me make it simple for you. I will summarize the terms of the will, and then I'll give each of you a copy of the document to take home, for your records. Does that suit you?"

We all nod in agreement.

My brother Giuseppe, even though he is younger than me, will inherit the family house on 12 Hayward Street, so long as my mother can live there the rest of her life. The lawyer calls it a "life estate," a kind of promise she can live there forever. I've never heard of such a thing, but it seems like a clever way of leaving my mother well cared for. A guaranteed roof over her head without the responsibility of ownership or having to make any decisions herself.

Of course, I am not surprised my brother gets the house. Property, as I was always told over and over, is passed down from father to oldest son.

My sister Mary receives five hundred dollars. That is more money than I thought my father had, stashed away in a bank savings account. The bank passbook has been held at the lawyer's office for safekeeping, and the money will now be handed directly to Mary.

Now it is my turn. I wonder what kind of money my father has set aside for me, his oldest child. If he has five hundred dollars to give to my little sister, I am guessing much more, maybe twice that amount, will be set aside for me.

"And to you, Celia, your father has bequeathed the sum of ten dollars."

I stare at him, waiting for him to continue. Something else will have to be added to this sum, some special gift or bequest for his first-born child. It must be ten dollars and... something else.

"Excuse me, sir. I think you read that number wrong. You mean a thousand dollars, not ten, no?"

"No, my dear. The sum is ten dollars. It is a nominal amount, to be sure, to let you know he did not forget you."

I turn to my mother, confused and hurt. "Why, Mamma? Why? Didn't Papà love me?"

"Of course, he loved you, Celestina. But he sees you living in that big house, on a plot of land three times the size as ours. You have a good husband and strong children to take care of you. You will never go without. Your sister Mary is young, just starting out in the world. She needs the money more than you do."

At this, my back and shoulders begin to stiffen, and I feel my pain turn to rage, a burning that swells in my chest and rises to the back of my throat, exploding from my head like a torrent of fire aimed directly at my sister.

"You? You get our father's love, and not me? You, who stole my childhood, while I changed your filthy diapers and my own baby's diapers besides?

"And you, Mamma, you remember how I nursed you in bed, waiting on you hand and foot, because having a baby at the age of forty was too much for you?

"Well, now I'm the one who's forty, with a baby at home, and another one on the way!"

My mother gasps.

"Yes, another hungry mouth on the way. And who is taking care of me? Who is allowing me to languish in my bed, while someone brings me little trays with cookies and tea, the way I did for you? No one! No one!"

I storm from the office and begin walking home, paying no attention to my unbuttoned coat flapping in the cold December wind, my face burning. I throw open the side door and burst into the kitchen where all my children are assembled around the table, playing cards, waiting to hear my good news about the will. They are not prepared for what I have to say.

"Five hundred dollars! That's what my sister gets. Five hundred dollars! And what do I get? Nothing! After everything I did for them. Nothing for me! Nothing for my children! Nothing!"

I tear off my coat and hat, throw them onto the floor, and kick them out of my way. I am about to retreat up the stairs, but before I do, I turn back into the kitchen and look at my children one by one, as they sit in stunned silence.

"From this day on, you will not speak to my sister. If any one of you ever, ever speaks to Mary again, I will cut off both of your hands!"

Stefano, 1927

Celestina tries to hide the papers from me, but I always find them. They never have any good news about my old friend Ferdinando, the one they now call Nicola Sacco. I don't know why I bother to read them anymore.

From the time of his arrest with his friend Bartolomeo Vanzetti, some seven years ago, I have carried this dread as if it were a noose around my own neck, waiting for the hangman to drop the trapdoor beneath my feet. I feel I am dying every day he is in jail. It's too much. Too much.

I will tell you a secret. I never told my Celestina, but sometimes, I used to sneak away to go to Nando's trial. My wife would be furious if she knew. I couldn't go every day because Celestina would suspect something. But I was absent just long enough so I didn't make her suspicious. Sometimes I told her I was taking some work on Molinari's farm to make a little extra money. Sometimes I told her I had to take the horse and wagon out of town for supplies. I always came back with something in the wagon to make my story look good.

I was there in 1921 when the death sentence was proclaimed by that monster, that Yankee judge—I can't even say his name. I don't want the poisonous taste of it in my mouth. It was a hot July day in 1921, and yes, I was there. There was such a crowd in the courtroom that I had to stand outside in the hall. I couldn't hear everything the judge was saying, but I could hear Nando's unmistakable voice cry out, "I am an innocent man!" It was a shout of rage and anguish that ripped a hole in me.

The crowd was in an uproar. I heard a woman in the crowd scream, "It is death condemning life!" Reporters running to telephones. Cameras flashing. Moans, sobbing, people wailing. I was pushed along by the crowd, and somehow, all the noise went silent. I could hear nothing. As if carried along by a strong river current, I found myself transported to the street. I felt like a ghost, floating. I saw people's mouths moving, but I didn't hear a sound. Somehow, I made my way home.

That's when the march of death began. The lawyer's appeals. Protests raging all around the world, in every country, it seems. And all the high-minded declarations from white-haired men, insisting my friend had a fair trial, filling up every newspaper with lies. That judge turns down every request for a new trial.

That is a man I could kill with my own bare hands.

Their latest lawyer, Michael Musmanno, takes on the case with the fervor of a saint. He files motions and appeals, stacks and stacks of paper, enough to go up to the moon and back. He goes all the way to the Supreme Court of the United States. But no one will listen.

Even when Nando's cellmate on death row, Celestino Madeiros, admits he was part of a Providence gang that committed the crime, that he was the one who killed the security guard, not Sacco and not Vanzetti, no one listens. The judge has made up his mind. He refuses to grant another trial based on this important new evidence that should have cleared my friend's name without any doubt. And the final appeal to the governor of Massachusetts is met with ice and steel. He is deaf to the lawyer's pleas.

So many years in jail are bound to make any man a little crazy. In 1923, they brought in these people called alienists to examine Ferdinando and see if he was insane. They declared him fit to stand trial. Bartolomeo is declared mentally fit a year later. I was hoping the two men would be found crazy so they could escape their fate. I am wondering who these men are and what makes them think they can judge a man's mind in such a short time. I'm sure they aren't working for the benefit of the two prisoners. They have other masters.

I would not be surprised if Nando and his friend Bart are descending into madness. Here in my house, I can feel it, as if connected to my old friend's pain by an invisible umbilical cord. I feel my descent along with them. In July of 1927, the two men go on a hunger strike, hoping to die before the electric chair can claim them—a final act of defiance. I want to starve along with them. I refuse my wife's good food night after night and prefer instead to find nourishment and comfort from my wine cellar.

The daily drum of news reports becomes unbearable, teasing me with false hopes one day before smashing them to bits the next. I keep hoping the lawyer Musmanno will discover some new angle or evidence or find someone with the voice of wisdom and reason, someone who might listen to his pleas.

In the end, none of it matters. The wheels are in motion. The almighty powers want those two Italians dead. Their prospects are fading like the newsprint their stories are printed on.

Celestina, 1927

I know how much they hate us, these Yankees with their plain white wooden churches and their cold Protestant faith, who look at our ancient Roman Catholic religion like something practiced by voodoo witches and savages. But I never thought it would come to this.

Now I read about the Ku Klux Klan planting a great burning cross just up the street from us, on Bear Hill, a monstrous thing to intimidate the Italians. I try to keep Stefano from reading such things. I don't think he can handle it. They burned another cross on Courtland Street, this one just like the first, all wrapped in burlap and soaked in gasoline before they set it on fire.

I know all about the KKK, too, and the big meeting they had in Worcester, with 15,000 people showing up, all too eager to become members and join arms, marching shoulder to shoulder with each other.

Stefano doesn't need to know any of that. But if he doesn't find the newspaper himself, one of his friends will tell him. Or one of his children.

I swear all my children to secrecy. I make them promise to say nothing to their father about the news of Ferdinando. But Cesarina—I call her Chezz—she doesn't have a brain in her head. You tell her not to tell a secret, and that's the first thing she'll do. She will use the secret like money to buy good favor from her father. She doesn't think about how the news will hurt him, only of advancing her standing as his trusted confidant. Selfish and short-sighted girl.

I know whenever Stefano hears a discouraging news report. That's when I find a few extra empty wine bottles under the grape arbor, or even in our bedroom, rolling around under our bed. The sour stench of wine on his breath, on his clothes, is impossible to miss.

I now regret ever giving him that glass of wine after his brother's passing. Now it is his only source of comfort. That, and the faint hope that his friend's execution will be put off one more day.

The month of August is tense. You can see it in people's faces all over town. The Boston & Albany Railroad Station, the granite quarries, and most of the big factories are patrolled by armed guards. It feels like we are in a time of war. The armed guards will stay and remain visible until Sacco's execution. The bigwigs worry that Sacco sympathizers will do harm to their precious properties.

Then comes the day I have been dreading for years. I fear it will drive the final nail into my Stefano's coffin.

August 22, 1927. *The Milford Daily News* evening edition carries the chilling headline that is so important, it runs across the entire width of the paper: "CONDEMNED MEN EXECUTED." Nicola Sacco, Bartolomeo Vanzetti, and their guilty friend Celestino Madeiros breathed their last breath early that morning, each one strapped to the electric chair in the Charlestown State Prison. When I read the headline, staring up at me from the kitchen table, my heart sinks. I call out for Chezz. She skulks into the room from the nearby parlor.

"You didn't tell him, did you?" The guilty look on her face is all I have to see.

"You stupid girl! *Cretina!* Where is he? Where is he now?"

She doesn't answer, too frightened by the rage in my eyes. I storm through the house, calling my husband's name. I run outside, to the grape arbor, the shed, the outhouse, the barn. He is nowhere to be found.

I walk down the street, calling, "Stefano! Stefano!" I feel sick, fearing he will do something foolish. I start toward the railroad tracks behind the Sacred Heart Church, thinking he might be lying across them, waiting for an oncoming train to end his life on the same day he lost his friend. Yes, that is something he might do. He would see something poetic in that, to be joined in death with his friend.

As I hurry towards the railroad tracks, I see a familiar figure slumped on the ground in front of the house on Mount Pleasant where Nando once lived. It is Stefano, loudly sobbing and moaning. All around, I can see curtains pulled opened and nosy neighbors sneaking a look at the scene.

I help my husband to sit up.

"You need to come home, Stefano. There's nothing to be done here. You must come home."

"They killed him. They killed him."

"It's over, Stefano. Please. Get up onto your feet. I'll help you."

I can see traces of red wine forming a purple outline around his lips. By the grace of God, I summon all my strength and lift my husband to his feet, but I can't keep his limp body upright. By now, my son Jerry has come looking for me, and he sees me struggling with Stefano. Jerry helps me keep my husband on his feet, putting one of Stefano's limp arms over his shoulder, and I pull his other arm over my own shoulder. The two of us drag Stefano back to the house, his feet stumbling and tripping along the street.

When we get to the house, my daughters are waiting and rush to help us—all but Chezz, who wisely stays out of my sight. We carry him up the steps into the house, as he flails and moans pathetically, and we get him onto a small sofa in the parlor.

"Someone get him some coffee," I yell, as I arrange him on the sofa and loosen his shirt collar.

"They want to kill us," Stefano moans.

"What are you talking about?"

"The police, the judges. Everyone. They hate Italians in America. They hate us. Nando was right. They're going to kill us. They're going to kill us all."

Jerry, 1928

My mother sometimes catches me looking at the cars advertised in the *Milford Daily News*. She says, "No one needs a car. Such foolishness. Big pile of metal, moving too fast. Enough to kill somebody. We have our horse. A horse is a noble animal!"

I don't argue with her. There is no changing her mind on anything. My father still drives a horse and wagon, long after Model Ts started taking over the streets of Milford. But the more my mother condemns cars, the more I want one. She is proving my point. The horse and carriage represent the old way, my parents' way. Part of a world gone by.

The day I get behind the wheel of a car will be the day I'll start to feel like a real American. The year I was born, 1907, is the same year Ford and General Motors started churning out cars for ordinary people. That makes the Model T the same age as me. And what could be more American than a Ford Model T?

I can remember being crazy for cars at the age of twelve. It was my first year at the Stacy Junior High School. I spent most of the school day staring out the tall windows onto Spruce Street, looking at the cars going by. I was so bored and restless sitting in a classroom all day, tapping my feet, twiddling my thumbs, listening to teachers I didn't think were any smarter than I was. I could read books without someone telling me how.

I quit school that year. That was as far as the law required. My big sister Lizzie left school after the fourth grade, but that was before the rules changed. I think she was the lucky one. I had to keep going to school three more years. One year at Stacy Junior High School was enough for me.

I think my father was more than happy to have me home all day and helping him full-time with his farm work. I also tagged along to help him doing odd jobs for his friends.

Once I was in my twenties, I decided I need a job with steady wages. It was all part of my grand plan: to save up enough money for a car. That's all I cared about. I didn't have much trouble getting a job at Draper, and so I became the second Marenghi generation to work there. But I managed to do better than the iron foundry, where my father worked. I got a job in the receiving department, loading boxes of metal parts needed for making textile looms. It wasn't long before I was promoted to a new job that had me driving my first vehicle—an electric jitney.

These are the machines that move people and things from one end of that sprawling factory to the other. I loved the feel of a steering wheel in my hands, warm and grooved underneath to fit my fingers. I loved the motor humming and vibrating under my thighs. Learning to take the corners smoothly, picking up speed when I have a clear aisle ahead of me. A feeling of flying.

I have to have my own car now. It is time.

It's a used Ford Model A roadster. Oh, how I love that car. I stare at it for hours, studying the curve of the fenders that seem to be floating like eyebrows over the spoked wheels. The headlights mounted like two bug eyes above the front grill, wrapped in shiny chrome cups. The canvas roof. I even love the spare tire mounted on the back.

Finally, I feel like a real American. I am a man with a car.

Having a car changes everything. I need a proper place to park it, and the dirt driveway that runs along the side of the house just won't do. An unpaved driveway is fine for horse and buggy but not for a heavy modern car. The wheels will get stuck in the mud in the spring. So I get to work making a paved ribbon driveway—two long runners of concrete pavers and a grass strip down the middle.

Now we need a garage. I picture a handsome garage big enough to hold two cars at the end of our new driveway, painted chocolate brown with white trim to match the house. My father taught me everything I know about carpentry when I helped him build a new barn some years ago. But I expect I'll be building the garage without my father's help.

He's not much of a help to anyone these days. Lately, he seems to be slowing down. And it's easy to see why. He lost his favorite niece and his brother the same year, back in 1920, and his best friend Nando was on death row for seven years. Every day for seven years, he worried it would be Nando's last. That took a heavy toll.

The final blow was his friend's execution. That almost did him in.

He spends more time in his wine cellar than anywhere else. Honestly, I can't blame him. I think he's earned the right to take a few swigs every now and then, after everything he's been through. My mother isn't very happy about it. But she's never happy about anything.

When the garage is complete, I find I don't want to put my car inside. Most of the time I leave it out in the driveway, for all the neighbors to see and admire as they pass by. I keep it so clean and polished, the sun glinting off it could blind you as you walk by.

My mother is amazed at my industriousness. And it's all because of my car. I want my house to be worthy of this beautiful piece of machinery.

As I think about the new garage and driveway, all shiny and new, it occurs to me that they make the house look shabby by comparison. I tell my father I want to improve the house he built. After twenty years, it needs some sprucing up. My father shrugs and says, "Do what you like. I'm done with building things. It's your turn." I replace the plain white columns on the front porch and add carved white balustrades. I add some new bay windows on both sides of the house. It looks very fine on the outside, and they bring more space and light to the hallway and parlor.

My father likes to watch me work and throw in his two cents. He is a tough audience as I install our first indoor bathroom with a flushing toilet tucked under the stairs to the basement, and then a shower stall and sink nearby. I also work on the kitchen in the back of the house, laying down shiny red-and-white linoleum squares on the kitchen floor, like a giant checkerboard, covering the old nicked and stained wooden flooring.

Now it is a modern house, truly worthy of standing next to my car.

―――――――――

Owning my first car is like getting the keys to the whole world. Every road, every highway, is open to me. I can go anywhere. I'm not limited by the streetcar's route or the distance my feet can take me. On Saturday mornings, I take long drives by myself on the back roads to Vermont, hunt for deer in the deep evergreen woods, camp by a lake, and eat fresh-caught trout for my supper. Getting away from a house full of sisters, I can find some peace.

I shoot mostly small game—rabbits, quail, a ring-necked pheasant or two. Every now and then, I drive home with a white-tailed doe strapped over the hood of my car. It causes heads to turn, driving along the country roads with a deer as my hood ornament. It puts meat on the table for days, with plenty left over to share with our neighbors.

Sometimes my sisters give me the evil eye—the *malocchio*—as my car pulls up to the house on a Sunday afternoon. They have to work, cleaning and cooking in the house and tending the gardens all weekend, while I am off doing whatever I want.

I try to make it up to them. On warm evenings, I put the top down on my old Ford and drive them around the neighborhood, all of us piled one atop the other. Chezz sits in the front seat with her accordion, Irene in the back plays guitar, and the rest of us sing as loudly as we can as I drive slowly up and down the streets of the Plains.

"Oh, I don't want her, you can have her, she's too fat for me – HEY – she's too fat for me – HEY – she's too fat for me…"

The neighbors must think we're drunk, but we're not. We are young and without a care. We are not afraid of being seen and heard. I love the freedom of moving anywhere I want, anywhere, any time.

Our Good Name

My brother Albert is never among us. The first-born child and a son, he always behaves as if he were in a higher class than the rest of us. That's what comes from being told your whole life that the oldest son inherits everything, as if it were the natural order of things, just as my Uncle Pietro had inherited the family land in Italy. Everyone knows Albert will get the house on Hayward Street, even though I put more labor and love into the place than he ever did.

Stefano, 1930

I am too old to be bringing another baby into the world. But my sturdy Celestina was about to have her eleventh child. I tell her we should have a doctor this time, or at least a midwife because she isn't so young anymore. But she won't hear of it. Stubborn to the end.

"I've done this ten times already. I can do it myself."

Louis came into this world on April 3, 1930. We name him after Celestina's father. He is a tiny little thing, all wrinkles and bone. And he is a boy. Finally, another boy, after five girls in a row. My father had too many daughters, just like my brother Pietro. But this little man is the one I have been waiting for. Another boy to carry on the family name and take care of my wife and my house when I'm gone. A boy.

Like an unexpected guest, he arrives in my house sooner than we planned. But he doesn't stay very long. The next day, Louis is dead. I think it is my last chance to hold a son in my arms. Back when baby Attilio died, I thought I could swallow my sorrow because we would have more children, more sons. This time, I don't think so. This is what my heart tells me, but I don't want to listen.

Celestina stays in her bed and doesn't want to talk to anyone, so I make all the arrangements. I buy Louis his own little gravestone in St. Mary's Cemetery, a little gray slab with a praying baby angel carved on the front. It made me cry when I first saw it. That praying angel tugs at my heart, because I was praying for a little boy.

After Louis dies, my Celestina is a different woman. Her eyes always cast down. Never smiling, never saying very much. The wife I used to know always recovered from hard times quickly. If the good Lord did something to knock her down, she would pick herself up and get on with her life. Not this time.

I come upon her in the kitchen one afternoon. She is rapidly slicing vegetables on the cutting board. She is like a machine, as if the tap-tap-tap of the knife has her in a trance. She keeps her eyes on the cutting board and not at me, as if I am not here. Her blank expression tells me she is lost in a deep sadness. I try to comfort her, standing behind her and gently wrapping my arms around her while she works. I tell her, "Everything will be fine, Celestina."

Holding her this way makes me think about all the times I used to come up behind her while she worked in the kitchen. Seeing her do little kitchen chores always used to excite me. That's when I liked to pull up her skirt and enter her from behind while she braced herself with her hands on the table. She always protested that the children might walk in and see us, but that only inflamed me more, made me push harder and faster. Remembering those times has an effect on me. Suddenly, I feel the familiar stirring in my pants, and she feels it, too. She turns around sharply and shoves me away from her.

"*Che fai?*"

"Celestina, *per favore*."

"No, Stefano. I won't. I have just buried my third baby with eight more still living. *Basta così!* I am done! No more!"

I know what she really means to say. No more in the kitchen, no more in bed. No more sliding up her nightgown in the night.

"From now on, I sleep alone!" she says. "You sleep in the parlor!"

"No!" I shout, stomping my foot. "I will not! I am the king of this house! I will sleep in my own bed, not be locked out of my room like a dog!"

"You are a dog! Always humping and poking me like an animal."

"You are lucky to have such a manly husband! I am strong. I am a man. I will sleep in my own bed, and I will take pleasure in my wife any time I want to!"

"If you do, I will cut off your *cazzo* in the night!"

I flinch at the thought and instinctively cover my manhood protectively with both hands. I pause for a moment and consider whether she is bluffing. I can see she is not. I notice the knife she is still gripping tightly as she stares at me with a look in her eye that would stop a charging lion in its tracks.

"Maybe I will find someone else to warm my bed," I say, trying to put a brave face on my defeat. "Yes, that's what I'll do. Someone young, fresh, and willing. Maybe a pretty little redhead like Nando's wife Rosa."

At this, Celestina's eyes grow large and her nostrils flare. This is when I know enough to walk away in a hurry. I retreat to my wine cellar. As I open a fresh bottle, I can hear Celestina stomping on the floor above my head.

"Go ahead, drink, you stupid fool! Drown yourself! Choke on it! I wish you were dead!"

I don't want to go upstairs ever again. I want to die right here in the cellar. But it gets colder and colder as the hours pass. I have nothing to sit on here but an old wooden chair. I get down to sit on the floor when the seat gets too hard, and back to the hard chair when the floor gets too cold. One by one I hear my sons and daughters come home and the sound of kitchen chairs scraping the floor under the supper table. I hear sounds of conversation, movement of people and chairs. Gradually the sounds fade to silence.

When I don't hear any more noise above my head, I think everyone has gone to bed, and it's safe to go upstairs and find a soft chair to sleep in. I sneak quietly up the cellar stairs and see the house is dark.

Ah. Much better. It's good to sit on my favorite armchair, alone in the dark, and pour myself another glass of wine. But I hear someone coming down the stairs. I know the steady thump-thump-thump sound of Celestina's footsteps. I close my eyes so she will think I am asleep. Maybe she will not yell at me if she thinks I'm asleep. I can't stand it when she yells at me.

She tugs gently on my arm. My eyes remain closed.

"Wake up, *amore mio.* Here, let me take that glass. Yes, that's it. You don't want to spill it. Come, I will help you. Up, up. Come to bed. I didn't mean to say all those things. Come to bed."

I open my eyes and see a ray of moonlight through the window peeking out behind a cloud, casting a soft light on my Celestina's face. She looks like a young girl in the light, her hair loose around her face, her white nightgown billowing like a soft blouse. I let her help me to my feet.

She holds my arm as we climb the stairs together.

Lizzie, 1932

It's a bright Saturday afternoon in late spring. I am working with my sisters Chezz, Irene, and Tillie in the gardens, tending to the young green shoots of gladiolus.

My papà always set aside most of his land for growing vegetables—tomatoes, corn, summer and winter squash, lettuce, radishes, flat romano beans, swiss chard, carrots, onions, basil, flat-leaf parsley—most of it for our dinner table. But in recent years, my papà had also ploughed and staked two long rows just for growing gladiolus. This is a different kind of garden, a cash crop.

Later in the summer, my father will set out tall milk canisters in front of the stone wall on Hayward Street, each one carrying a different color bunch of gladiolus. Red, yellow, orange, white, pale pink, and even shades of purple and dark burgundy. They are so colorful; you can't miss them if you walk or drive by, and it is easy and tempting to stop and pick up a bunch for fifty cents a dozen.

I'll tell you what I think. I can't stand those flowers. They mean nothing to me but back-breaking labor from spring to late summer. To make it worse, my papà sits all afternoon in the shade of the grape arbor, with a jug of his home-made wine at his feet, pouring glass after glass until his lips turn purple, getting meaner and drunker by the minute.

"You missed that weed over there, Lizzie! What's the matter with you! I can see it from here, and you can't? You don't have a brain in your goddam head. And Chezz, I don't want to look at your fat ass in the air. Face the other way. No one wants to look at that."

That isn't the papà I grew up with. He used to be a sweet man with comical loose pants and suspenders, an Alpine felt hat, and a fuzzy moustache that tickled my cheek when he kissed me. He used to be such a cuddly man. Now he is just plain mean. A mean drunk.

I don't know what happened to him. His cheeks are hollow, his cheekbones sharp. Barking out swear words from one side of his mouth and orders from the other, barely able to stay balanced in his chair without falling over. My sisters and I look at each other sympathetically as we bend over the young plants. I whisper to the others, "Don't pay any attention to him. It's the wine talking. Just keep working." I always thank God when my mother calls out the window, telling us to come inside for supper.

My mother's hot minestrone doesn't cheer me, nor the good crusty bread from Mazzarelli's, nor the salami she made herself and had hung to dry in our attic. Nothing she sets on our table makes me hungry anymore. I only eat out of force of habit. I know my father will soon come stumbling in and snarl at everyone at the table, shaking all the dishes and glasses as he lumbers to his place. I put food in my mouth, but I can barely taste it.

On Monday mornings, it's almost a relief to go work in the factory after putting up with my father all weekend. These days, I am working at the Lapworth factory making elastic straps and bands for women's underwear. The boss is an Englishman, very upper-class, very full of himself, and a mean son-of-a-bitch. He has nothing but contempt for the Italian women who keep his factory humming and put money in his pocket. But he is actually a prince compared to my father.

Sometimes, I wish my old man would just die and put us all out of our misery. I know I shouldn't think about my father that way. But I can't help it. That's how I feel.

Jerry, 1934

I wasn't surprised when Albert married Lucia Testa, after dating her for two years. They have a house of their own now on 30 East Main Street, close to the Sacred Heart Church. He has been doing alright for himself. He has a good-paying job, making almost nine hundred dollars a year, driving a truck for the Curtis Coal and Ice Company. His wife, just twenty years old when he married her, works at Milford Shoe. With no children yet and two incomes, they have money to spare. They have everything.

And Albert always has nice cars. My Ford Model A was already an old used car when I bought it, and I've been driving it more than ten years. Long ago, I learned to take care of a car, how to take it apart and put it back together, so I can make it last forever. But Albert somehow finds a way to buy a brand-new car every two years. Studebakers. Plymouths. Fords. Sleek lines and chrome grills, and creamy pastel colors that make everyone stop and stare.

My old Model A has spoked wheels, while Albert's cars have silvery hubcaps. My car is black from top to bottom, dented and more than a little rickety, with visible patches of rust. Albert's cars are always as slick and shiny as the day he drove them home.

I'm itching to buy a new car, and now's the time to do it. Prices are dropping on everything. Gas, electricity, and basic bread and butter— you name it. Eggs that used to cost fifty-five cents a dozen now cost thirty-five.

It's hard to figure. On the one hand, I hear about hard times, people jumping out of windows because they lost everything in the stock market crash. But those are people with stocks and bonds. I don't know anyone like that. I wouldn't know what a stock looks like or where to get one. Most people I know don't even have bank accounts.

And if there's some kind of industrial depression happening, it's hard for me to see it. There are two new shoe factories in town—Friendly Shoe Company and Lyons & Hershenson—joining the ones we already have. F. W. Woolworth bought space in downtown Milford and built a brand-new store. And the town has seen several big construction and highway projects in recent years. New cement sidewalks edged in Milford pink granite run the entire length of town. And just a couple years ago, we had a parade to celebrate our new $100,000 Main Street.

I think the automobile is changing our town. I'm not the only one in love with them. Cars are replacing horses, trolleys, and trains. In 1928, we see the last of the electric street trolleys, when the Grafton & Upton Line between Milford and Grafton makes its final run.

I'd like to have a new car someday, but for now, I'll settle for a used vehicle. And I find a real beauty. A black Plymouth with modern rounded lines and real hubcaps. One of the hubcaps is missing, but at least it's newer than my rickety Model A. This car isn't just nicer on the outside. Inside it has real upholstery, as nice as living-room furniture. This car won't just convey me from one place to another. It is obvious to my father what this car can do.

"Now that's a car you can catch a woman with," my father tells me. "You're almost thirty. You should get married, like your brother did."

But I am in no hurry to do anything my brother did.

"Women don't want a man with a car, Papà. They want a man who can give them a nice house. A mink stole. Money in the bank."

"Then do it! Don't wait till you're old and no one wants you anymore."

The truth is that I prefer the company of men. I love fishing and hunting, the quiet pleasures of the great woods of New England. I like men I can wander with in the woods for hours and hours without saying a single word. Sitting at the edge of a lake with a smoke in one hand and a fishing pole in the other.

Women don't like to do these things. They like to talk all the time. Talk talk talk. They want men in nice clothes to take them out to restaurants, bars, theatres. I don't like fussy clothes, and I am not a fan of closed spaces filled with lots of people, trying to make small talk with too many voices chattering around me.

I like the sound of my own silence.

Celestina, 1937

If only you could have seen my poor husband, Stefano, the day I brought him to the exorcist.

That's right. An exorcist.

I got the idea from the Catholic priest who heard my confession. On trembling knees, I told him I was thinking bad thoughts about Stefano. I said I wanted to divorce him. I know priests don't like to hear that kind of talk, so it took all my courage to say so.

For five years after the death of our last child, Stefano's drinking has worsened. He is no longer any help to me, or even to himself. The kitchen is my domain, and the wine cellar is his. I manage everything from my kitchen table while my husband is directly below me, sinking further and further into hell.

I tell the priest that Stefano's drinking is killing my family. He is full of demons, tormenting my children with poisonous words that seem to be coming from someone else, some foreign voice, an evil presence inside of him. The sweet old man my children always knew is no more. He scolds and insults them.

The priest's face was hidden from me, but his instructions were clear. He told me what I must do. Not a penance of saying the Hail Mary ten times. Nothing like that. He told me to come to his office, to talk with him privately. There he explained exorcism to me. Only a Catholic priest can do it. He knows the right words to speak to the demons. He will command the demons to leave Stefano's body. And then Stefano will be restored to his former self.

He told me about a secret house in the North End of Boston. I cannot say the names of the people who gather there. I am sworn to secrecy. I do what the priests say—they are wise in such matters. They are arbiters of all things that move on Heaven and Earth. They administer the lightning bolts and the thunder. One must listen to them.

I will take my husband to the house where they summon demons and extract evil spirits. To make Stefano go there, I must tell him a big lie. I say we are going to Boston to buy his favorite muscat grapes from the pushcart vendors in Haymarket Square to make more wine. That's what I tell my children, too.

"It will do your papà a world of good, a change of scene," I tell them. "Good for his poor heart. And it will give you all a break from his nagging presence."

When we get off the bus in Boston, we walk to his favorite part of the city, Haymarket Square and the North End where all the Italians live. He isn't paying attention as I guide him to a dark alley where we have never been before, as my priest had directed me. There is a room at the top of narrow stairs and hallways that smell like burnt butter, stale cheese, and cabbage soup. An elderly woman dressed in black opens the door and lets us in.

The room is dark, save for some slivers of light that peek in between the heavy drapes. There are several older women dressed in black, sitting in wooden chairs arranged around a large, empty tufted armchair. It's an old and much-used piece of furniture, the grim gray upholstery worn down to mere threads in the seat. The arms of the chair are stained a darker color from so many human arms resting on them. I hate to think of what has gone on in that chair.

The seated women grip rosary beads in their hands and seem to be muttering to themselves. My Stefano is guided to the old armchair and made to sit. The poor thing seems confused. Maybe he thinks these ladies are friends of mine or relatives whose names and faces he has forgotten after all those many years of drinking too much. He looks like a child hopeful of receiving milk and biscotti.

When the priest enters in his long black cassock, Stefano gives a little start and seems alarmed. But the priest calms him with a soothing tone, holds his hands, and tells him not to fear. "You are now in God's hands," he says. "Soon, your heart will be at peace."

The priest begins to chant in Latin, and the women in the room murmur soft prayers. I am the one who is afraid now. I can feel tension mount as the priest's chants become louder and more urgent. I cannot stand it. I have to leave the room. I don't want to witness whatever evil is about to erupt from my husband's mouth like filthy bile. I don't want to see him in the clutch of demons who will wrestle with the priest for my husband's soul, a violent clash of wills, until one of them surrenders or falls dead.

I slip into hallway and pace back and forth on the small landing. The sunlight casts a strange light on the stairs from a small window. Shadows crawl up the steps and lengthen as the sun droops and the hours pass.

At last, the priest emerges into the hallway and tells me it is done. He takes my husband by the elbow and guides him gently down the stairs to the street below as I follow anxiously behind. Stefano squints at the intense late afternoon light.

"Take him home," the priest tells me. "His soul is free. He will suffer no more."

"So that's it? There's nothing more to do?"

I thought the priest might hand me prayers to recite to my husband. Or a list of herbs to boil into a tea to serve with incantations. Just a few hours to extract the demons from my husband's soul? They must have been very weak demons.

Stefano looks dazed and sleepy. The afternoon air is warm and soothing, and a cool wind is whipping in from the open sea. I think a walk to the harbor might revive him and lift his spirits before our bus trip home.

I lead him gently toward the nearby waterfront, walking along one of the long granite warehouses until we can look out at the open sea. We stand by the wooden pilings and look down into the brackish water below. I think I see jellyfish, billowing like ghosts, wearing sheer white skirts just below the water's oily surface.

"Look, Celestina," he says. "This is all wrong. The water should be blue, deep blue, like the Mediterranean, but here, it is dirty and brown. It has no color. Everything good has color. The yellow plums of Pereto. The deep green of good olive oil. But here, what do you see? No color in the water, just filth and poison and the reflection of a dirty gray sky."

Suddenly, I see a splash in the water. Stefano's hat is floating on the surface of the water, that old Alpine felt hat with a ragged feather, the one he wore on his voyage across the sea in 1895 and has been wearing each day ever since. The one I patched and stitched, whose lining I replaced a dozen times.

"*Cosa fai, pazzo?* Where are you going to get another hat like that?"

"I want it to float like a sailboat all the way to the Mediterranean Sea. I want it to carry my spirit home, all the way home, to join my dear brother. I want to go back and visit everything I have lost. I want my bones to sleep next to my mother and father."

And as I watch him staring at his hat bobbing on the waves, I know in that moment, my husband is gone from me.

Whatever that priest extracted from my Stefano, he went too far. He also removed whatever was left of my husband's will to live.

He has given up. The end of his life is in sight. From then on, he will float from day to day without purpose or direction, weightless, empty. In just a few short years, he will loosen his grip on this mortal world. But I alone know the real moment when his soul left him, on that day overlooking Boston Harbor, with his hat floating off to the open sea.

Lizzie, 1940

Papà is in a bad mood this Monday morning, worse than I've ever seen. He said he is feeling sick and can't get out of bed. I know what that really means. Another hangover.

My mamma insists he stopped drinking. She says a priest gave him a cure. She can think whatever she wants. Nothing on Heaven or Earth could make that man stop drinking.

I am sure he won't go out all day, just flop around in bed, making demands of my poor mother, shouting orders from his bedroom and making everyone run up and down the stairs to wait on him like a king.

On days like this, I'm glad I have a job to go to. I'd rather be standing on an assembly line all day.

With everyone fussing over Papà all day, I assume no one will have time to get the newspaper that afternoon. I stop to pick up the *Milford Daily News* on the way home from work. I can't believe the headline. It is the biggest blackest headline I have ever seen, all in capital letters, and it runs the whole width of the paper. It says, "ITALY DECLARES WAR!" Underneath that, a smaller headline says, "Mussolini Says Decision 'Irrevocable.' "

I don't know how to pronounce that word. Ir-re-vo-ca-ble. But I know it isn't good. It is shocking to see such a big headline. It seems to be screaming at me. There are articles on England and France and what they have to say about it. And it says President Roosevelt plans to speak to the nation that evening over the radio. Now I know what I'll be doing tonight. My whole family will be sitting around the radio after supper and listening carefully to Roosevelt's every word. I roll the newspaper up and tuck it under my arm.

I arrive home a little before five o'clock, walking in through the side door to the kitchen, expecting we will all have something big to talk about over supper. But instead, I find my family is crying around the kitchen table. My mother looks up and says, "Elisabetta! Where have you been? We tried to reach you at work today. But your boss said no messages were allowed while you were working. No messages allowed!"

What message?

My sister Chezz blurts out, arms flailing, as dramatic as an opera singer's performance, "Papà is gone! I was there at his bedside, holding his hand just before he passed. He was crying, Lizzie. He begged me, he made me promise, 'Don't let anyone take away our house! The house belongs to this family! Don't let anyone ever take away this house!' Then he sits up and takes a big gasp, and then falls limp and dead into my arms.

"*Grazie a Dio*, he is finally at peace," she adds, closing her speech with the sign of the cross.

I stop in my tracks, not knowing if I should feel grief at my father's death or shame for wishing it to happen. Maybe it is all my fault. I wanted him to die. I wished for it many times. And now this.

I cover my face with my hands in shame and start sobbing. "It's all my fault! It's all my fault!"

My mother rushes over to embrace me. "It's alright, my baby. It was his time, and God's will. It was not your fault."

"Isn't there something in the paper, Lizzie?" Jerry asks. He notices I have dropped the rolled-up newspaper on the floor. He picks it up and smooths the front page flat on the kitchen table.

There it is, a tiny article, just an inch high, on the bottom of page 1. The header said, "Stefano Marenghi Died Today." The headlines on the top of the page were so big and jarring, I completely missed the much more important news, the news about my father, hidden like a small lead weight that sank to the bottom of the page. It is just four sentences. He died at noon at his home. He was born in Italy. He leaves behind his wife and eight children, each one listed by name. He lived in Milford for forty-five years.

I never thought I would see my family's name in the newspaper. But it appears again just a few days later with a little column on my father's funeral mass at Sacred Heart. The paper names all the pall bearers: Domenico Volpicelli, Primo Bonatti, Eugenio Resmini, Joseph Volpicelli, Antonio Mongiat, and our cousin, Giovanni Marenghi.

My father would have liked this part. The notice says "a large number of mourners" attended the funeral. Isn't that what he always wanted? For his brother Pietro to know he had made something of himself in America?

A man with many mourners. A man of importance at last.

———————————

My father's death is a sadness, but a part of me feels it as a relief. A weight lifted from me, a nagging presence no longer pointed at me like a loudspeaker. My mother can be just as demanding as my father was, but she never had my father's problems with drinking. My mother never needed wine as a crutch.

She always had me.

It isn't until my youngest sister Rose is in her teens that I can finally break free from my babysitting chores and my mother's long shadow. I can finally think about having a man of my own.

His name is Emilio Taddei. I met him at the schoolyard. It has a set of swings that are quiet and empty on summer evenings after the children have all gone home. Sometimes I like to go there by myself after supper, sit on one of the swings, and let it rock me and rock me like a baby, listening to the chains on the swing creak and creak, back and forth, like a lullaby. It was a perfect place to catch a soft breeze, where I could be alone and at peace.

I see him one evening walking past the schoolyard gate, and he notices me sitting alone on the swing. He is wearing a white cotton shirt, short-sleeved and close fitting, showing off his strong forearms. His upper body is shaped like a triangle, wide at the shoulders, narrow at the waist. His dark hair is combed back smooth, heavily oiled and slick on the sides, leaving a mass of loose curls on top.

He walks past the open gate at first, and I am not sure if he noticed me. He then turns around and walks back casually and slowly, heading toward me on the swings, taking a seat on the one next to me, barely saying hello at first. He seems too shy to speak, but that never was a problem for me.

Before long, I get him talking. He tells me he's a shipping clerk at the Dennison company in Framingham, where they made paper boxes, labels, and tags. He works in the warehouse, moving and loading heavy boxes all day. Before that, he worked as a stonecutter at the granite quarry. I can believe that. He has the solid muscle of a man who knows something about hard labor.

I like that in a man.

The next thing I know, I am going to the swings after supper every evening, and Emilio is always there waiting for me. Before long, my nosy little sisters start to suspect something. They notice my frequent absences after supper. One evening, they follow me, all five of them, Chezz, Irene, Tillie, Catherine, and Rose, their sneaky heads peering up over the stone wall along the schoolyard. When I spot their bobbing heads, they suddenly duck back down, and I hear them giggling, followed by the rapid patter of their feet as they run home. I know they're going to tell our mother. Now I'll have to face all her questions about Emilio when I get home.

One evening, Emilio comes to my house to take me out to dinner at Carboni's. When he arrives at my door, he is carrying a big bunch of red gladiolus. Foolish man. He doesn't know any better. All I can think of is those big bundles of red gladiolus my father used to sell in milk canisters in front of our house and all the sweat and pain from my body that went into those big bouquets.

"What are you thinking, wasting your money like that on flowers? Tomorrow they'll be dead and in the trash. Don't you ever waste your money like that on me again!"

Poor Emilio looks wounded and slinks away with his bouquet. I don't know until many days later that he was planning to propose to me that night. I saw the flowers he had in one hand, but I didn't see the ring he had in the other. I'll bet he never expected that kind of reaction from me. I always have a way of saying whatever comes into my head. Talk first, think later. This time, my timing was very bad. I really hurt Emilio's feelings. But somehow, he forgives me.

By the time we are married, I am already a woman in my forties. Too old to be a mother, even though I was a mother to my sisters and brothers all my life.

If I ever thought for one minute that life would be any easier after I got married, I was mistaken. Marriage just gives me one more baby to take care of. I traded my mother's babies for one of my own. A grown man baby. As soon as we say, "I do," I find out that I'm the only one who does all the doing. Every day I do and I do and I do. He doesn't.

I don't know what it is about men. They seem so strong and capable when you first get to know them, but once that ring is on your finger, they turn into helpless little boys. My mamma tells me that's my fault. She says I'm the one who's breaking Emilio's spirit. I do too much for him. I make him soft. I don't let him be a man, she says. But what am I supposed to do? If I wait for him to weed the garden, the weeds will be up to my knees. So I do everything myself.

Sure, he goes to work every day. But I do, too. He gets to rest when he comes home from work. I don't. He gets to sit back and relax on a soft cushioned chair, kick off his shoes, and wiggle his toes. I don't. I'm still standing. I'm making his supper. The floors are just as hard where I work all day. My feet are tired, too. But I'm the one still standing.

I can't remember a day when I didn't go to bed with aching bones. I am always on my feet, whether it's in the kitchen or in gardens or on factory floors. Never a day of rest. Never a vacation. All that work has made my ankles swollen and my hands rough, my body as thick and solid as a tank. Good thing Emilio likes me built this way, but I don't. I think working like a mule has drained all the feminine softness from me, hardened my features and broadened my shoulders. Sometimes when I look in the mirror, I think I'm looking at a man.

If you ever pass me on the street, don't ever tell me to have a good day. I don't know what a good day is. I never had a single good day in my life.

Jerry, 1944

I never thought much about women until one day in 1944 I see a shapely form, a perfect hourglass, moving across the shop floor at Draper Corporation. She doesn't move in a flirty way, swinging her hips or strutting like a fancy bird. No, she is strong and steady, walking simply, as a man would walk. Her hair is dark and curled around her face, but she doesn't look Italian. Her nose is rounded and turned up, not sharp and angular like Italian women, and her rounded body is softly curved like the aerodynamic lines of my car.

And her eyes! They are a color I had never seen. A light green maybe, or a golden hazel? Their strange color gets my attention. One day, I speed up my jitney to take a closer look, and she jumps aside, as if she's afraid I was about to run her over. I didn't realize my sudden speeding toward her would frighten her, but she takes it well. She looks up at me in my driver's seat and gives me a good-natured smile. Such big white teeth she has! And such generous lips. Everything about her is full and rounded and curved.

I ask around and learn she works in the front office. She is a Mendon girl named Myrtle Thomas. I start waiting for her every night after work and finally work up the courage to say, "Hey, Toots, you wanna lift?" And what do you know? She hops into my car. She lets me drive her home.

It then becomes a habit, driving her home every night through the tree-lined back roads of Mendon, an old farming community where mostly Yankee families live. Sometimes I don't stop at her family's farmhouse and keep on driving past, driving around in circles, just to keep her near me a little longer. She seems as shy as I am, which I like.

A quiet, soft-spoken girl, raised on a farm. Not a spoiled city girl with up-town tastes and phony manners.

My family doesn't like this budding courtship, and neither does hers. My mother and sisters want me to find a nice Italian girl. They hope this Thomas girl will just be a fling—just sowing my wild oats— and that I'll eventually come to my senses. Her family, especially her mother, feel the same way. They want her to find a man from old New England stock with a good English name and good prospects. Italians aren't even human as far as her mother is concerned. Just criminals and bomb-throwers.

The first time I kiss her is in my car. It is a warm summer night in June, and we have the windows rolled down. I turn down a back road in Mendon and pull off the road onto a wooded dirt road where hunters sometimes park their cars. The woods are silent, with only an occasional rustling sound of wind through the trees, or maybe a fox moving in the brush. Myrtle's scent is driving me crazy. Not a smell of perfumes or powders, but an animal smell of sweat and heat.

In September, she tells me she is pregnant. It was only once that we did it in my car, but once was enough. I won't have the luxury of a long courtship to ponder how I feel or years to think about whether we should get married. I have to decide quickly.

My mother doesn't like it, but she tells me to do the right thing. "And if your father was alive, he'd tell you, too," she reminds me. Too bad my father died without ever seeing me getting hitched.

I buy Myrtle a ring. A diamond so small, you can barely see it, set against a shiny chrome disk designed to magnify the gem's size. Myrtle accepts it as if I have given her the crown jewels.

We get married by a justice of the peace, right before Myrtle's twenty-fifth birthday. Our honeymoon is a long weekend in a little cabin in the New Hampshire woods, on the edge of Lake Sunapee. Every morning, I wake her with the smell of frying eggs and bacon that I cook up over an open campfire.

On the long drive home, we talk about our plans. We want to build a good life for the child Myrtle is carrying. A better life than we had. We don't want to work at Draper for the rest of our lives. We want to build something that is ours alone. Isn't that what this country is all about? Chasing the American dream?

We are going to have a farm of our own. A flower farm. My Myrtle was always sweet on gladiolus, ever since she saw the ones my family grew on Hayward Street. And she's got a good head on her shoulders for accounting and bookkeeping. We are going to work the land, and it will reward us. We will be rich landowners someday.

We will scrape together all the money we have, a few hundred dollars, and buy an acre of land on the eastern edge of town. I know just the place. The street is barely populated and doesn't even have a name yet. I swear to Myrtle I'll build her a fine house, just as my father did for his wife. I'll cobble it together with my own hands, using any scraps of wood I can find, lumber that's discarded from construction sites, even old wooden pallets from the Draper loading dock.

Myrtle and I take a little apartment on East Main Street until our new house on the edge of town is habitable. When Marcia is born in 1946, followed by Celia in 1947, the apartment is getting smaller and smaller, but I am working on the new house as fast as I can.

Finally, it's ready.

At first glance, the house isn't much to look at. It's just a single room with a roof over it, a spring-fed well with a hand pump, and an out-house set back under the pine trees on the edge of the woods. There is no telephone, no central heating, no indoor bathroom, no kitchen cabinets, or closets. Not yet, anyway. It's just four walls, a big wood-burning stove, a deep kitchen sink, a table and chairs, and a big iron bed.

Myrtle tells me it's romantic, a cozy little cottage. But I promise her it is just the beginning. We'll add onto it as our fortunes grow, and before long, I tell her, we'll be living in a nicer house than the one I grew up in. I promise.

I feel good setting down roots on my own land, having my own house and car and a growing family. I keep working at Draper, while also turning that fertile black soil into a flower farm. Someday, all my labors will pay off.

I wanted to make a life my father would have been proud of. He would have loved my two little girls, especially Marcia with her curly red hair the same color as his. And then when Celia came a year later, with her black hair and dark eyes, she looked more like my sister Catherine. Celia and Catherine even share the same birthday, March 1.

In fact, it seems Catherine is the only one in my family who ever comes to visit us. Sometimes when I am out working in the flower fields, I see Catherine smiling and waving to me from a fancy car rolling down our long dirt driveway. Albert is at the wheel, showing off his latest new car, just to make me jealous. That's the way he is. And his wife Lucy always sits in the front seat, in the middle, sandwiched in between Albert and Catherine. But he and Lucy never step out of the car to visit with me or my family—they are only dropping off Catherine.

Myrtle loves Catherine, too. She is the only one of my sisters who is ever nice to her, and she never held it against her that she wasn't Italian. She lets Myrtle call her Kay.

Catherine loves to see my little girls. She helps Myrtle brush and roll their hair into banana curls and brings new dresses for them to try. Catherine loves to send the girls running down the path to the flower fields, where I'm working, to show off their new dresses for me.

When Jerry is born in 1952, you would think Catherine just had a baby herself. She can't get enough of my little baby boy, a chubby nine-pounder when he was born. Catherine is a frequent visitor, sharing our simple kitchen table by the wood-fired stove, bouncing little Jerry on her lap. She never minds or criticizes our simple one-room home, and she is never too proud to use our outhouse. She is twenty-five, a pretty girl with short black curls that bounce when she walks.

I hope to see her married before long. Anyone who loves children as much as Catherine does is bound to have a family of her own. It would be a crime if she doesn't. Some good man will have to notice her, maybe one of the many men she works with at the Telechron clock factory in Framingham. Plenty of Italian boys among them.

Even though I am nineteen years older than Catherine, I dream our children will play together one day. But 1952 changes all that. Changes everything.

Jerry, 1952

It is the first day of June, almost five months to the day after my first son was born. It is around midnight, and I am up late reading a true detective magazine, smoking a Camel, and just starting to doze off in my favorite chair when there comes an unexpected knock at the door. It's my nearest neighbor, Inez Taddei, with a raincoat pulled tight over her flowered nightgown and her hair in rollers. Inez is a single woman in her forties, sister to my brother-in-law Emilio, still living in her childhood home with her widowed mother. She holds an umbrella over her head, and a heavy rain is falling.

"What are you doing out there on a night like this? Come in, you'll get soaked."

"Jerry, I got a phone call from your mother. Your sister Catherine is at Milford Hospital. It's very bad. Very serious."

I don't wait for details. I grab my old cardigan sweater and car keys, tell Inez I'll drop her back at her house on the way, and head straight to Milford Hospital. I don't say a word to Myrtle, who is sleeping next to baby Jerry when I leave.

Inez says something about Catherine going to a drive-in movie that night with Albert and Lucy. I can picture the three of them in the front seat, as they always are when they're out together. Albert behind the wheel. Lucy in the middle. Catherine in the passenger seat. I don't know what they are doing out on such a miserable stormy night. All I can think was that they must have been in some kind of car accident on the way home.

When I get to the hospital, they tell me Catherine is in surgery. They direct me to a room where I find Albert and Lucy. Albert looks fine, not a scratch on him that I can see, but Lucy is in bed with a bandaged nose and bandages around her arm.

I demand to know what happened.

We were coming home from the drive-in. Crossing Route 140. A car slammed into us on the passenger side.

Were you speeding?

No, I wasn't speeding. It was raining hard. Could barely see. Driving very slow.

What were you doing out on a night like this?

It wasn't raining earlier.

What happened to Catherine?

Thrown from the car. Unconscious. Hurt pretty bad.

Why aren't you the one in surgery? Why are you sitting there without a scratch? Why does it have to be Catherine? Why isn't it you?

A surgeon enters the room, a tall man with a flat expression. He looks at each of us before he speaks. He is sorry, he says. Nothing he could do.

At this, I feel such rage, I turn to my brother and swing at him with all my strength. He ducks just in time, and the surgeon has to hold me back, grabbing me from behind, my arms swinging wildly. Interns and orderlies rush to his aid. Many hands are on me, pulling me away from Albert.

I want to kill Albert. And I say so. Loudly. I say it so many times, they have to call a police car to take me home.

All the way home, I'm banging my head against the patrol car window. Why. Why. Why did it have to be Catherine? Why isn't it Albert? Why is it Catherine? Why isn't it Albert? Why is it? Why is it why is it why is it why is it why is it?

———

The next day, the *Milford Daily News* tells the story. All I can see is Catherine's face staring up from the large front-page photo, her dark eyes looking directly at me. It is a story spanning multiple pages and covering every detail, including a diagram of the crash scene and a giant "X" marking the center of the intersection where the cars collided.

As Albert was driving home around 11:30 that night with his wife and his sister, he was heading east on Route 16, crossing the intersection of Route 140, when a drunk driver came speeding across the intersection, ignoring the stop sign. He hit the car squarely on the passenger side. The car spun and Catherine was thrown from the vehicle.

Albert's new Ford is a total loss. It had only a couple thousand miles on it, the reporter notes. Why is that so important? Is the reporter feeling sorry for the car? What does a car matter, anyway?

Myrtle tries to stop me from putting the newspaper into the fire, stuffing it down the top of the stove, but it's too late. She thinks I should save things like that. She likes to save everything in her cedar chest. But I don't want to be looking at that newspaper story anymore. I tell Myrtle I don't want any pictures of Catherine in the house, ever.

Catherine is laid out in a closed coffin in my mother's front parlor. Neither Albert nor I have the stomach to be her pall bearers. I can barely manage to attend the funeral at Sacred Heart, or the graveside service where they lower her into the family plot next to my father.

I never again love cars the way I once did. I soon sell my Plymouth and buy a cheap wreck of a car that has been crudely painted with flat green housepaint. Cars mean nothing to me now. Just four wheels to take me from one place to another.

I remember my mother's words. "No one needs a car. Such foolishness. Big pile of metal, moving too fast. Enough to kill somebody." She was right. She was always right.

I never speak to Albert again.

Part 3

The Next World

Celestina, 1957

You didn't know that I would ever die, did you? Well, some of us die. Some of us don't.

I left my body in 1957. But I am still here in this house on 7 Hayward Street. I hover through the rooms like particles of air, like steam from a pot of soup on the stove, like the dust that rides in beams of light and never settles anywhere.

I am here. I can see all of you, my children. And you, Stefano, my dear departed husband, suspended in time beneath the grape arbor, pale as the frost on withered vines. Even the ones not yet born. I see you all.

I have no plans to die. Ever. I am watching all of you. And how I love getting the last word!

Of course, I planned well for my death. I never forgot the power that my father's last will and testament had. I was resolved to have a will of my own. Stefano died without a will, but he could barely think straight in his final days. It was up to me to ensure our affairs were left in good order.

For years I had been doing a lot of thinking about my children. I watched them, studied them, thought about which of them would inherit everything I had built over a lifetime with my husband. Stefano was no longer around to tell me that the oldest son gets everything, as every Italian family has done since the dawn of time. I was the one writing the will, and I would make my own rules. I would decide what to do with everything.

Me. Not him.

I found a nice Jewish lawyer, Nate Rosenfeld, and told him the story of my children. He needed to draw a map to keep all the names straight. I told him about Albert, my oldest, the first of my children to marry. Albert did okay for himself. Nice home, nice car, and a much younger wife. He did not need anything from me. And he would get nothing in my will. What a surprise this will be. I can't wait to see the look on his face when he finds out. Because my spirit will be there, in the lawyer's office, watching my children when the time comes for the reading of my will.

I tell Mr. Rosenfeld how one by one my other children follow Albert's lead and get married. I was mother of the bride five times after Stefano passed away. Lizzie, Jerry, Chezz, Tillie, and Irene were all married after the war ended. I was sure my youngest girls, Rose and Catherine, would not be far behind. But then Catherine had to leave us so suddenly.

"And grandchildren?" my attorney asks. Oh, I had a few complaints about that. I had to wait many years for my first grandchildren. How could so many children of mine produce so few grandchildren? It's a disgrace. *Che disgrazia!* But I waited. I needed to see grandchildren before I wrote my will.

Jerry's first child was Marcia, born in 1946. That same year, Irene gave birth to a daughter, and later, Albert also adopted a daughter. But Jerry was the first to give me a male grandchild who was not only my own blood, but who also carried the family name. Jerry's namesake was born in 1952. I remember thinking, finally! This is the one I was waiting for. Baby Jerry will be destined to carry on our family's good name.

Finally I could die.

This is why my son Jerry has a special place in my heart. But Jerry doesn't get the house, either.

I tell my attorney I want to bequeath my house and everything in it to Jerry and Myrtle's children. This way, the house and land will remain in the hands of a Marenghi for as long as possible. It would be just like the villages in Italy, where the family lives on the same plot of land for centuries. The same church that holds a child's baptism record holds the birth, marriage, and death records of her great-great-great-grandparents, generation after generation, digging their family roots deeper and deeper into the same soil each year.

And those life estates I learned about with my father's will? I will grant one of those to my son Jerry and one to Lizzie, Chezz, and Tillie. These three daughters, all of them childless, did the most to take care me as I grew older, and in return, I will give them and their husbands the right to live in my house as long as they want. But the house will never be theirs. Jerry's children, my grandchildren, will get everything.

I have always been able to divine the future, and I see it even more clearly now that I have crossed over to the other side. Jerry's wife, Myrtle, will be like me, bearing children over many years. She will produce three girls and three boys from that thick, strong body of hers, her bones as broad and deep as a cradle. And the seeds of our family name will live on, like the cherry tree my husband planted, heavy with wine-colored fruit year after year.

Albert won't be happy about any of this, and all my girls won't like it, either. Especially Tillie and Chezz, the ones who nursed me in my final dying days. After they married, Tillie and Chezz moved with their husbands to Vermont, where they started an Italian restaurant, the Gulf House, in Williamstown.

That's where they sheltered and cared for me when my body weakened with age. That's when the abscess on my neck swelled with all the pus and rage of everyone who ever wronged me. The last remnants of tuberculosis, lingering undetected in my body over decades, waged its silent war on my heart and lungs. And uremia, when my kidneys failed me, caused piss and waste to collect in my blood. The final blow was the stroke that shut the blood supply to my brain, stole my words, and silenced me on earth for good.

I took my last breath on June 17, 1957.

Yet, I am still here in my house, watching over my family, judging them, guiding them, even if no one can see or hear me. I was watching as they lowered me into the ground beside my husband Stefano in the

Sacred Heart Cemetery. I watched my oldest daughter, Lizzie, wailing loudly over my coffin, as she did at every family funeral. And wouldn't you know, as soon as I was buried in my grave, I saw Lizzie leaning on the shoulder of my sister, Mary Speroni, the one I told my children never, ever to speak to again or else I would cut off their hands.

Lizzie and Mary would become great friends after I was gone. Ungrateful witches, both of them.

At last came the reading of the will in my lawyer's office. I was so looking forward to this, to watching from another world, my spirit ballooning over the room like a fluttering canopy. Albert, Lizzie, Tillie, and Chezz were there. I grinned at the shock on their faces when they learned not one of them inherited my house. Ha! Now they know how I felt at the reading of my father's will. Instead, everything went to the one family that was not present at the reading of the will. Jerry, Myrtle, and their children.

I knew Jerry wouldn't be there. He never ventured out of the house if he could avoid it, not even to hear the reading of his mother's will. He didn't like to be around people anymore. After his sister Catherine died, he wasn't the same. He quit his good job at Draper's after twenty-five years of working there, the same year he lost his sister. After that, he spent most of his time in his gardens.

For some men, like my husband, comfort came in a bottle. For Jerry, it was growing flowers. But his gladiolus farm didn't do very well. In the early 1950s, no one was buying gladiolus anymore. For years, everyone loved gladiolus, the flower of romance and sweetheart bouquets. They were seen everywhere, in magazines, in the movies, always elegant displays in fan-shaped vases. Next thing you know, you couldn't give them away for free. Gladiolus became nothing more than cheap filler flowers used in funeral baskets.

The farm Jerry worked so hard to build had failed. He had no work, no prospects. He was silent, morose. He liked doing things that required no talking—like fishing and hunting or grafting new varieties of apples onto his prized apple tree. How many kinds of apple do you need on one tree? But that's the only kind of work he liked to do. Solitary labor. Like my Stefano, he also took frequent comfort in the body of his wife, and she bore him children until she was in her forties, just as I did for my Stefano.

Maybe Jerry's final straw was the day they buried me at the Sacred Heart Cemetery, with Stefano's coffin on one side of me and my daughter Catherine's on the other. I think that pushed Jerry over the edge. He couldn't take any more death and loss. I thought an exorcist might do him some good, like the one who worked on Stefano. Instead, he went and checked himself in at the mental clinic for poor people in Boston, the same one that took all the shell-shock victims from the war. The Southard Clinic for the Indigent Mentally Ill.

They used electric shock therapy. I'm not sure that was any improvement over exorcism. A lot more primitive, if you ask me. Jerry went there for many treatments, but I can't say it helped him get back on his feet. He never had a good-paying job again. The St. Mary's Parish felt sorry for him and gave him odd jobs, like fixing the toasters and unclogging the sinks for the nuns in the convent. They also made him the cemetery caretaker at St. Mary's, where he mowed the lawns and dug graves. That wasn't very good for his mind, for a person broken by too much death to take up work as a gravedigger.

Not much of a life.

Maybe that's why Jerry didn't show up for the reading of my will, never knew the special place he had in my plans. He could have lived in my big house the rest of his life instead of suffering in that pathetic little shack he built on Prairie Street. That's where he died in 1964, his heart giving out in his sleep, on his own big iron bed. He looked like an old man, with his white hair and grizzled beard, but he was just fifty-six years old.

Jerry went to his grave without ever forgiving Albert for driving the car that killed Catherine that night. Poor fool. He even named his next child after her, little Catherine, a plump pink thing with golden red hair just like Stefano's.

I have my eye on that granddaughter. She will be blessed with the education my children never had, and she will become a woman of letters one day. I will sneak into her head and plant an idea to write a book about me, so I will live forever in the mortal world as well as the hereafter. She will think it is all her idea, but it's really mine. She will be a warrior, defending the family honor. She will never give up her name, Marenghi, our most precious inheritance. I will sharpen her tongue like a knife to defend our good name.

Someday, she will know everything. I have faith in her.

The House, 2022

Ah, my dear Celestina. You think you got the last word? I don't think so.

Houses speak. Houses have memory.

I am the house on 7 Hayward Street. Like all the people who have crossed my threshold, who gave birth here, who died here, I have a life. I have a voice even if two-legged mortals choose not to hear it.

I speak many languages. I speak the northern Italian dialect of the carpenter who built me. I know every Italian dialect that permeated every house in my neighborhood. I picked up the Quebecois of the cottage behind me, a language I learned from the French Canadians who once rented it. I know the plain raw English of immigrants learning their adopted country's language. And I know all the houses around me. We talk among ourselves.

We talk about the human detritus that lurks in the wood and fiber of our bodies. Hair follicles, flakes of flesh, effluents from childbirth, soil tracked in from gardens, filaments of wool and cotton, crumbs of bread, drops of wine. Torn and water-stained pages from movie fan magazines stapled to the walls of my attic. An old scrapbook, forgotten in a corner of the cellar, its spine held together with string. Artifacts that fell through cracks in my floorboards, like the black-and-white photo of Chezz and her friends in a nightclub in 1944. She never knew what happened to that picture. But I knew.

There was a time when I was abandoned, homeless. How can a house be homeless? When it is not lived in and loved. My fate was sealed when Celestina bequeathed me to her son Jerry's children. Somehow, this legacy was cruelly kept secret on obscure legal parchments for decades. Neither Jerry nor his family were aware of their good fortune and continued to live out their lives in the shabby one-room structure that he built. Such a waste.

I don't blame Chezz and Tillie for being angry. They wanted to inherit the house. They tried many times to sell me, but they couldn't get a clear title. Celestina's last will and testament prevented that. Out of sheer spite, they invested nothing in maintaining me. In the end, the sisters gave up on trying to sell me and simply walked away. They abandoned me.

Weeds took over my pretty gardens. Passersby tossed trash into my untended yard. A peach tree took root under my porch, and its branches pushed through the planks of my porch floor. My dark brown paint faded to a sickly red and peeled from my flanks. White paint curled and crumbled from my pillars and moldings.

I was ashamed.

When assessors came to inspect my abandoned shell at the start of the twenty-first century, they found me as I was, looking like a pitiful old dowager who couldn't afford to buy new clothes for many years. My kitchen had an old-fashioned cupboard instead of proper cabinets, bare patches of floor where ancient appliances once stood, and a frayed gingham skirt around my massive kitchen sink. Window shades were torn to shreds. My light switches had old-fashioned pushbuttons; most people replaced those with toggle switches by the 1950s. My plaster walls were cracked with fine lines like crow's feet. My cellar had hundreds of empty wine bottles lying on their sides on deep wooden shelves, many spilling onto the floor, and dried-out dregs still rattled inside them. It looked like the aftermath of a party that no one bothered to clean up.

The heirs to my ruined body didn't know what to do with me. I was nearly a hundred years old. They all had homes of their own by now, homes that were younger and prettier than I was. They saw no choice but to sell me to an investor who was undaunted by the massive restoration and facelift I required. He had no emotional ties to me. No sentimentality. He just wanted to pretty me up for a quick sale.

Now I wear white vinyl siding like a cinched plastic raincoat over my tired old walls. My guts have been reconfigured into apartments. I'm not nearly the grand lady I once was. My gladiolus gardens and grape arbor are long gone. Frankly, I'm offended by the paved parking lot where the Bing cherry tree once stood. Even worse, a second building has cropped up right next to me on this same property, and I don't like the way it's crowding me. We are not on speaking terms.

Meanwhile, the human languages that sputter over the airwaves and pierce my vinyl walls are changing daily. Italian and English are now peppered with Spanish, Portuguese, Arabic, and an occasional dash of Chinese. I even detect exotic tongues like Quichua, spoken by Ecuadoran tribes. Why the newcomers keep coming to this fading industrial town is hard to say.

We, the houses, simply shrug. We have seen and heard it all. We have watched generations of newcomers plant themselves on this inhospitable soil. They come running from the clutches of hunger, poverty, and fear. But they are never welcomed. Not even the children of those who were once immigrants themselves will extend a welcoming hand to the newcomers. As if one person's desperate flight to America was more righteous and pure than that of his new neighbor.

I will outlive you humans, both the newly planted and the deeply rooted. But even so, I know these pillars and beams won't last forever. If the elements and termites don't get me, the wrecking ball will. Eventually. But until I am knocked to the ground and carted away, I will remember all the beautiful names of those who passed through my doors.

Stefano. Celestina. Bartolomeo. Elisabetta. Girolamo. Cesarina. Irena. Matilda. Caterina. Rosa. And all the other short-term tenants of this world.

Like the forgotten names of a million migrating birds.

Acknowledgments

This book is a work of fiction. All the people and places actually existed, but the stories are entirely imagined.

Our Good Name would not have been possible without the support of the good people of Milford, Massachusetts. Some of them are historians and researchers by trade, including Anne Berard of the Milford Town Library, Anne Lamontagne of the Milford Historical Commission, and local historian Dan Malloy, who maintains the fabulously helpful website, www.hopedale1842.com. I am deeply grateful for all their help.

Many of the most valuable and treasured resources are family and friends who graciously offered their time and interest. My cousin Frank Speroni and his wife Lucy often invited me into their Milford home, where I heard Frank, a man in his late nineties, share his lucid and fascinating remembrances of my family. Frank is the son of Mary (Abretti) Speroni, and my grandmother's nephew. My cousin Debbie Ferrari, who shares a great-grandmother with me, Marianna Abretti, told me the story behind the phrase "death rides a bicycle," which I found remarkable.

My deepest gratitude goes to the Volpicelli family, who gave me the most direct insights about my grandfather's home village in Italy and maintains strong ties with the people there. They include Celestina Volpicelli Kopech, her mother Giovanni Volpicelli, and cousin Gino Cordani. All of them lived in and around Milford, Mass. Our families were linked when Albina Marenghi married Domenico Volpicelli in 1907.

Special thanks go to Steve Minichiello for his unflagging friendship and support and for sharing with me both family lore and his priceless collection of letters that he compiled from his Milford ancestor Caterina Zurlo Iannitelli, written from 1906 to 1936. Likewise, Anthony Allegrezza kindly shared with me a written history of his own ancestors, the Baldelli family. Ross Mazzarelli shared personal stories of his Milford family, and Marc Cenedella traded stories with me about his ancestor, Giacomo Cenedella, the *padrone* who assisted Italians like my grandfather in migrating to America.

Other fabulous Milford resources included Angelo "Chuck" Calagione, my former civics teacher, who happened to have once lived in the former home of Nicola Sacco. He sent numerous valuable documents my way, including a Harvard University bachelor's degree thesis by Nicholas Mastroianni, Jr., which detailed the history of Italians in Milford. The Bontempo family was exceptionally gracious, including the brothers Giancarlo and Michelangelo and their mother Evelyn Bontempo. She, along with Chuck Calagione and many others, attended a talk I gave on Italian immigrants at the Milford Historical Commission in 2019, and she shared with me the wrenching story of why her family emigrated to the U.S., which I used as an epigraph in Chapter 2. (When she asked her father, "Why did you leave Italy to come to America?" he answered, "When you're hungry, straw doesn't fill your stomach.")

I am grateful to Fil Melendy, a Milford neighbor of my grandparents and aunts, for sending me a scrapbook belonging to my aunt Rose Marenghi, with newspaper clippings compiled in the 1940s.

Spencer Sacco, grandson of Nicola (Ferdinando) Sacco, was kind enough to respond to my emails. He confirmed for me that it is quite likely his grandfather went by the nickname Nando, short for Ferdinando.

Louis Risoli, my friend of many years, shared valuable stories on his ancestors in Gropparello, a town not far from my grandparents' native home. While visiting that area in 2019, I made the acquaintance of Caterina Perotti, a retired schoolteacher who graciously gave me an impromptu guided tour of the villages of Metti and Pereto, part of the municipality of Bore. Caterina introduced me to Pino Resmini, a longtime resident of Pereto, who shared local lore and showed me the sites where my grandfather Stefano and my great uncle Pietro probably lived. Caterina also later agreed to edit my Italian chapters for cultural accuracy. For that I am very grateful.

The March 1927 issue of *The Atlantic* carried a superb account entitled "The Case of Sacco and Vanzetti." The article's transcript of Sacco's testimony is printed almost verbatim from that excellent article in Chapter 22 of this book.

I am supremely grateful to Ann Black, managing editor of Arch Street Press and the guiding light behind the making of this book. Her editorial insights, suggestions, and comments were always spot on and deeply incisive. She listened to me, challenged me, and made this book better. Thank you, Ann, for placing your faith in me.

And my son, Steven Pfau, a fine writer and editor and the most voracious reader I have ever known, is always my listener, my advisor, and my inspiration.

Thank you, all.

Selected Bibliography

Bencivenni, Marcella, *Italian Immigrant Radical Culture: The Idealism of the Sovversivi in the United States, 1890–1940,* NYU Press, 2011.

Frankfurter, Marion Denman and Jackson, Gardner, editors, *The Letters of Sacco and Vanzetti*, Penguin Books, 1997.

Hixon, Linda and Farren, Christian, editors, *The Grip: The 1918 Pandemic and a City Under Siege*, Second Edition, Dutcher & Ellsworth, 2021.

Program Committee of the Sesquicentennial, *Milford, Massachusetts 1880–1930: A Chronological List of Events for Fifty Years,* Charlescraft Press, 1930.

Tejada, Susan, *In Search of Sacco and Vanzetti: Double Lives, Troubled Times, and the Massachusetts Murder Case that Shook the World,* Northeastern University Press, 1912.

Unattributed, *New York Times*, "First Strike in 97 Years: Draper Company Experiences Only Walkout in Its History," April 1, 1913.

Various authors, *The Milford Daily News*, 1895–1945, archived on microfiche at the Milford Town Library, Milford, Mass.

Author's Notes

While *Our Good Name* is a work of fiction, many of the stories were inspired by a combination of family lore and historical events. The following notes provide additional context.

Marianna, 1910

- **The Massilia.** Marianna recalls her transatlantic voyage on the Massilia, confirmed by Ellis Island ship manifests. The same ship gained notoriety in 1892 when it was blamed for a typhus epidemic in New York City. Sailing from Marseilles, France, on January 1, 1892, with 270 Jewish passengers, refugees from Russia, the Massilia then stopped in Naples, Italy, to pick up 457 Italian passengers before heading to New York. A subsequent outbreak of typhus in New York City was traced back to the overcrowded ship, and it set off a wave of anti-immigrant feeling nationwide. Immigrants were blamed for bringing disease and crime into the United States. [Source: Cannato, Vincent, *American Passage: The History of Ellis Island*, HarperCollins, 2009]

- **Census of 1910.** The U.S. Census reported in 1910 that members of the Abretti family on 6 Hayward Street, Milford, included a son "John" whose age was recorded as "zero." This John was actually Marianna's grandson, the infant son of Mary (Abretti) and Louis Speroni, born in 1910 and residing at the same address. I imagine the character Marianna in my book, overcome with grief over her lost son, may have been confused by the John named in the U.S. Census as being her son John with "zero" years of age and having "no years."

- **Death rides a bicycle.** It is family lore that Marianna did not wish any of her children or grandchildren to ride bicycles after losing her son in the bike accident. The phrase "Death rides a bicycle" was attributed to her by one of her great grandchildren, my cousin Debbie Ferrari.

- **Restaurateur.** Marianna predicts that her daughter Maria will one day own "a *trattoria*, a nice restaurant, and feed all the people in town." The adult Mary Speroni, a fine cook in real life, fulfilled this prophecy.

The Speroni family owned and operated a popular Italian restaurant named Speroni's in Medway, Massachusetts, for more than fifty years.

Stefano, 1879

- **Rosso.** Stefano Marenghi as a boy is nicknamed Rosso because of his red hair. Sometimes Rufo, Ruffo or Ruffino are variants of this nickname, derived from the Latin "rufus" meaning red. Rosso literally means "red" in Italian, used here to simplify understanding.

- **Donkey Story.** The story of the donkey that contracted tetanus, was killed on doctor's orders and buried, only to be dug up later for food, is based on a tale told directly to the author in 2019 by Pino Resmini in the village of Pereto. It was also recorded as local lore in a modern history of Bore by Linda Marazzi. It is not known if the Marenghi family directly participated in this feast, but it is likely considering the small size of the village. [Source: Marazzi, Linda, *Bore: Arte, Storia e Natura*, Pro Loco Bore, 1994]

Maria Rosa, 1880

- **Mondine.** While there is no evidence that Maria Rosa Marenghi, the protagonist of this chapter, was a *mondina*, it was highly likely. Tens of thousands of women worked as migrant farm workers in the northern Italian rice paddies from the mid-19th to mid-20th century. The author heard personal accounts of this work from the Volpicelli family, which is related by marriage to the Marenghi family. Both families come from adjacent villages of northern Italy. Giovanna Volpicelli, a Milford, Mass., resident, gave the author a first-person account of being a young *mondina* in the 1940s, providing vivid details from memory. Another member of the Volpicelli family, Gigino Cordani, related the story of a male rice worker who died from an infected cut on his hand. Today the labor of these manual weeders has been replaced by commercial herbicides and automation.

Stefano, 1882

- **Marenghi Maglie.** It is not unusual to find many unrelated families with the same surname in Italian villages, thus giving rise to the practice of nicknaming different families to tell them apart. Irma Marenghi, granddaughter of Pietro Marenghi, related the story of the Marenghi Maglie nickname during the author's visit to her village in 2019.

Celestina, 1908

- **Sexual assault.** There is no evidence, either historical or anecdotal, that Rosina Marenghi, the niece of Stefano and Celestina Marenghi, was sexually assaulted by her factory boss. However, there is ample evidence that immigrant girls and women endured widespread sexual abuse at the hands of factory bosses in the early 20th century. The story is included here to illustrate the victimization of young female factory workers, especially immigrants. "In the early 20th century, women employed in new manufacturing and clerical positions confronted physical and verbal assaults from male supervisors. Union leadership was successful in enacting protective legislation that shielded women from performing physically demanding labor, but not from the propositions of lecherous bosses. By the 1920s, working women were advised to simply quit their jobs if they could not handle the inevitable sexual advances." [Source: Cohen, Sascha, "A Brief History of Sexual Harassment in America Before Anita Hill," *Time Magazine*, April 11, 2016.]

Stefano, 1910

- **Ferdinando Sacco, AKA Nicola Sacco.** The man remembered as a martyr in the Sacco & Vanzetti trial of 1920 was indeed a resident of Milford, Mass., from 1910 to 1917. Although they were nearby neighbors, there is no evidence of a close friendship between Stefano Marenghi and Ferdinando Sacco. The friendship is fictionalized here to illustrate the parallel experiences and tribulations of two Italian immigrant families. Sacco was well known in Milford, and many residents would have followed the trial with deep interest. To this day, Sacco is still spoken of affectionately in the town, described by many as a gentle soul. Sacco's grandson Spencer Sacco confirmed that Nando would have been a likely nickname for Ferdinando before he changed his name to Nicola. Fifty years after the two men were executed, Governor Michael Dukakis of Massachusetts declared by formal proclamation that "the atmosphere of their trial and appeals was permeated by prejudice against foreigners and hostility toward unorthodox political views," rather than based on "the weight of the evidence." Dukakis ordered that "any stigma and disgrace should be forever removed from the names of Nicola Sacco and Bartolomeo Vanzetti, from the names of their families and descendants, and so, from the name of the Commonwealth of Massachusetts." [Source: Proclamation of Nicola

Sacco and Bartolomeo Vanzetti Memorial Day by his Excellency Michael S. Dukakis, Governor, August 23, 1977.]

Stefano, 1912

- **Guido Mazzarelli, Hopedale.** The anecdote of Milford baker Guido Mazzarelli being prohibited from making bread deliveries in the town of Hopedale, Mass., was told to the author by the baker's descendant Ross Mazzarelli.

Celestina, 1913

- **Emilio Bacchiocchi.** The tragic story of Emilio Bacchiocchi, who died in a labor union strike against the Draper Company, of Hopedale, Mass., is well documented in the *Milford Daily News,* archived at the Milford (Mass.) Town Library, and also extensively documented on the invaluable history website www.hopedale1842.com, curated by local historian Dan Malloy.

Celestina, 1920

- **Pietro Marenghi's death.** The actual year of Pietro's death was unclear as of this writing in 2022 and is estimated between 1911 and 1920. The year of Pietro's death is not indicated on the Marenghi family tomb in Bore, Italy, and was difficult to confirm due to shifting jurisdictions over the town's vital records. The author chose 1920 as his year of death for its impact as a literary device—one of three tragic events or "dark angels" that visited the family in the same year, 1920.

Ferdinando, 1920

- **Testimony.** Nicola Sacco's actual testimony at his trial, in broken but poignant English, is slightly condensed but taken almost verbatim from the trial transcript published in *The Atlantic* in 1927. It is used in Chapter 22 of this book. [Source: Frankfurter, Felix, "The Case of Sacco and Vanzetti," *The Atlantic,* March 1927.

Celestina, 1926

- **Luigi Abretti's will.** Celestina's outrage over feeling short-changed in her father's will, and her threat of "cutting off the hands" of her children if they ever again spoke to her sister Mary, was related to the author by Mary's son Frank Speroni. The author fictionalized the notion of "life estates" as being a part of Luigi's well, but it was an actual feature of Celestina Marenghi's final will.

- **Lynching Italians.** Stefano rants in this chapter about how Italians are not perceived as "white" and are threatened by lynchings. The author is aware of the sensitive nature of this topic. In no way does she mean to suggest that immigrants endured worse treatment than people of color. Blacks in America have been murdered in thousands of documented cases of lynchings. However, the lynching of Italian immigrants is not fictional. On March 14, 1891, perhaps the single largest lynching in U.S. history involved eleven Italian immigrants in New Orleans, Louisiana, who were accused of murdering a local police chief. After they were acquitted in a jury trial, an angry mob of thousands, shouting "hang the dagoes," used battering rams to storm the city jail. Eleven Italian men were riddled with bullets and dragged outside to be hanged on public lampposts. A *New York Times* editorial praised the lynching as a warning to other Italian "criminals." On March 21, 1891, Theodore Roosevelt, then serving on the U.S. Civil Service Commission, wrote this in a letter to his sister: "Monday we dined at the Camerons; various dago [SIC] diplomats were present, all much wrought up by the lynching of the Italians in New Orleans. Personally I think it rather a good thing, and said so." The experience of immigrants was nowhere as horrific as what Blacks endured for centuries, but it is true that white supremacy and racism has directly affected Italian immigrants. [Source: Staples, Brent, "How Italians Became 'White,'" *The New York Times*, October 12, 2019]

Celestina, 1927

- **KKK cross burnings in Milford.** The activities of the Ku Klux Klan (KKK) in Massachusetts are well documented. In 1925, *The Washington Post* estimated there were more than 370,000 KKK members across New England, and many "sundown towns" prohibited both immigrants and people of color from appearing on the streets after dark. In the early 1920s, Klan meetings and cross-burnings began to occur with some regularity in small towns in eastern and central Massachusetts. Cross-burnings targeted Catholic Irish, French Canadian, and Italian immigrants as well as people of color. In Milford, Mass., cross-burning incidents are cited in the Program Committee of the Sesquicentennial, *Milford, Massachusetts 1880–1930: A Chronological List of Events* *for Fifty Years,* The Charlescraft Press, 1930. They are also reported in *Worcester Telegraph and Gazette,* October 18, 1924. [Source: New England Historical Society website, www.newenglandhistoricalsociety. com]

Jerry, 1934

- **Exorcism.** Reports of Celestina's consulting both exorcists and witches are part of Marenghi family lore. The exorcism described in this chapter is undocumented and fictionalized in this book. Stefano's tossing his hat into Boston Harbor is also part of the family lore.

Celestina, 1937

- **Same day reporting.** It may surprise some modern readers to learn that newspapers typically published several editions a day during the first half of the 20th century, nearly rivaling the speed of modern electronic reporting. The death of Stefano Marenghi was indeed reported the same day that he died on June 10, 1940 in the *Milford Daily News.*

Jerry, 1944

- **The car accident.** Details of the car crash are true and carefully documented in the *Milford Daily News.* The author witnessed the fact that her father Jerry and his brother Albert were not on speaking terms for years. Her conjecture is that the animosity was a grudge over Albert's driving the car that night of the fatal accident that killed their sister Catherine.

Someone has to make it out alive, sang a grandfather to his grandson,
His granddaughter, as he blew his most powerful song
into the hearts of the children.

—Joy Harjo, "How to Write a Poem in a Time of War"

Catherine Marenghi is the author of the memoir *Glad Farm*, which President Jimmy Carter said was, "An inspiring story of a writer and journalist who overcame great handicaps to achieve success." She is an award-winning poet with two Academy of American Poets prizes, among others. Her work has been published in North American and international literary journals. Her chapbook, *Breaking Bread*, was published in 2020. Her first novel, *Our Good Name*, was published in May 2022.

The granddaughter of Italian immigrants, Catherine writes with a profound sense of place and a keen interest in where we come from and how we define home.

Catherine was born and raised in Milford, MA, a town where she has deep roots and a lifelong connection. She is an active member of the vibrant literary community of San Miguel de Allende, Mexico. She has served on the board of the San Miguel Poetry Cafe and, with poet Judyth Hill, co-founded the Poetry Mesa, an international community serving poets and poetry.